MILO MOSS IS OFFICIALLY UN AMAZING

MILO MOSS IS OFFICIALLY UN AMAZING

LAUREN ALLBRIGHT

LITTLE, BROWN AND COMPANY

New York Boston

Little, Brown and Company
Hachette Book Group
1290 Avenue of the Americas, New York, NY 10104
Visit us at LBYR.com

First Edition: September 2020

Little, Brown and Company is a division of Hachette Book Group, Inc. The Little, Brown name and logo are trademarks of Hachette Book Group, Inc.

Library of Congress Cataloging-in-Publication Data
Names: Allbright, Lauren, author.
Title: Milo Moss is officially un-amazing / by Lauren Allbright.
Description: First edition. | New York : Little, Brown and Company, 2020. |
Audience: Ages 8–12. | Summary: Milo and his parents desperately want to win a Guinness World Record, but Milo ultimately discovers what winning really means.
Identifiers: LCCN 2019051216 | ISBN 9780316428774 (hardcover) |
ISBN 9780316428781 (ebook) | ISBN 9780316428750 (ebook other)
Subjects: CYAC: World records—Fiction. | Winning and losing—Fiction. |
Family life—Fiction. | Middle schools—Fiction. | Schools—Fiction.
Classification: LCC PZ7.1.A4375 Mil 2020 | DDC [Fic]—dc23
LC record available at https://lccn.loc.gov/2019051216

ISBNs: 978-0-316-42877-4 (hardcover), 978-0-316-42878-1 (ebook)

Printed in the United States of America

LSC-C

10 9 8 7 6 5 4 3 2 1

TO MIMI
(I LOVE YOU SOOOOOO MUCH.)

CHAPTER 1

My favorite story from the Guinness World Records is about a tiny piece of land in the middle of the ocean. Somewhere close to Great Britain exists Bishop Rock. It's only the size of about three tennis courts. And it's known as the SMALLEST ISLAND WITH A BUILDING ON IT.

The story goes like this: A long time ago, ships would be drifting through the waves—open ocean as far as the crow's-nest guy could see. The crews of the ships would be thinking they were in for smooth sailing as they were swabbing decks, walking planks, carving new wooden legs and whatnot. Then, without warning, *BAM!* They'd ram into this tiny, nonthreatening, no-big-deal island—and their boat would splinter into toothpicks.

It kept happening again and again until some higher-up, like a queen or king, was like, "We have far too many toothpicks and not enough boats because of that silly island! We must fix this. Go forth and build a lighthouse!"

So they hired some dude to build that lighthouse. For three years, the guy and his crew worked to construct it out in the middle of the endless sea. Sunscreen wasn't even invented yet. Or porta potties.

Over *one thousand* days later, the work was done. A 120-foot-tall lighthouse stood on this itty-bitty island in the middle of the great big ocean. But before they could even have a grand-opening celebration, something went wrong. A big wave came up and—*whoosh*—washed the lighthouse away.

Just like that.

Splash.

Gone.

All before they even lit it up.

So the guy gets to work again and designs something better. This time it takes him and his crew years and years to build. He makes sure this one is super waveproof.

Nearly three thousand days later, that lighthouse is finished. This is the one worth noting. This one is called the "King of Lighthouses," and it gets the island in Guinness.

I love this story so much because I get it. All the stuff that happens "before" is okay because eventually it *wins*. The lighthouse outlasts the waves. The island gets a record.

This is what gives me hope.

Someday my parents and I will get a record too.

And that day is today.

Which is why we are currently in the car dressed as human-sized cockroaches.

CHAPTER 2

Since it's September, the newest edition of Guinness has just been released. Thank goodness I have that to read because the view outside the car window is scraggly trees, brown grass, and endless cacti.

I'm halfway through the animal section—the mantis shrimp wins the award for the STRONGEST SELF-POWERED STRIKE BY AN ANIMAL with a kick equal to 340 pounds of force—when Dad says, "Hey, Milo, how about you read some of those records out loud?"

"Or Mom could do it," I suggest.

"Nope," Mom says from the front seat. "*Mom* was up late painting roach wings, and she is currently sleeping. It's *your* turn to entertain our driver."

"Safety laws frown upon reading and driving at the same time," Dad says. "Come on. At least just read page ninety-six."

Translation: Dad doesn't really want me to read from the Book. He's just wants to talk about the "real" Iron Man, Richard Browning—the guy who invented a flight suit and got into Guinness.

"Whoa, Dad. Did you know the largest yo-yo was almost twelve feet tall?"

Dad ignores my comment. "How fast did Browning fly again?"

"And that yo-yo weighed four thousand six hundred twenty pounds!"

"What was his flight speed again? Can you remember, Milo?"

I flip some more pages. "Can you believe the tallest toothpick sculpture is almost seventeen feet?"

"Milo," Mom says. "Just tell your father what he wants to know. You're interrupting my beauty sleep."

Dad pats her knee. "You don't need that, honey. You're already stunning. I bet Richard Browning would think so too."

"Milo!" Mom says.

There's no escape. I resign to my fate. "The real Iron

Man, Robert Browning, flew eighty-five miles per hour in a body-controlled jet-engine suit."

"Really?" Dad says like he is shocked. He's not. Dad knows everything about Browning. "And how did he power that suit?"

"With six kerosene-fueled micro gas turbines," I quote from memory.

"And I bet it could go even faster than that." Dad knows it could. "Don't you think?"

"If only it had a parachute."

Richard Browning is actually really cool. He worked on the flight suit for years, but he only recently got into Guinness. And now he is Dad's hero—maybe it's because they're both engineers and marathon runners. Or maybe it's because Browning has done what Dad has always dreamed of: Richard Browning has earned a world record.

Because I am an excellent son, as I flip through the pages of my new Guinness, I also listen to Dad talk about Browning and how there will be a day when flight suits will be as common as cars. I supply the appropriate "uh-huhs" whenever he pauses.

When Dad starts talking about all the flight-suit proto-types, my nose starts to twitch. A tickle builds inside my left nostril. I force it into the loudest, most intense sneeze of my life.

Seriously *that* could have been a record.

In the front seat, Mom bolts upright.

Success!

"Whew." I scratch my nose. "Sorry. Didn't mean to disturb you, Mom. It's just something really irritated me."

Mom slowly turns to glare. "Something is very irritating to me too."

"Now that you're awake though, you should hear what Dad was just saying about how we'll all have our own flight suits someday. Go on, Dad. Tell her."

Mom crosses her arms. "Milo's fortunate that we don't have a flight suit right now. Or that's how he'd be getting to Shotwell Stadium."

Dad sighs. "If only we were so lucky."

CHAPTER 3

It's lunchtime when we get to Shotwell Stadium in Abilene, Texas, where we'll earn a Guinness World Record for the largest crowd of people dressed as insects.

Mom, Dad, and I double-check our costumes. Once our long antennae, slip-on bug bodies, and extra legs are all in place, we grab our sack lunches and trudge through the parking lot. We stop at the check-in table in front of the main entrance.

My heart beats hard inside my homemade thorax. We're here on time, we made it with no flat tires or car breakdowns, and our costumes are accounted for. Registration is the last step. After this, nothing can stop us.

Just past the gates, the place is already crawling with participants. Mom and Dad finish at the table, and my family gets the okay to join the rest of the crowd.

I let my parents go first, and I pause to absorb the scene—the stadium, the people, the last moments before everything changes.

Inside, Mom stops and studies the map she grabbed when we checked in. "Let's follow along the backside of the bleachers. When we get to the corner at the end, there'll be a ramp down to the field."

"Lead the way," Dad says.

It gets harder to stay together as the swarm of people-sized bugs gets thicker. We veer around giant butterflies and spiders and somebody in green who I think is a grasshopper. The plastic roach wings on my back make me sweat. I stop to lift them and get a little airflow. This is a mistake. It cools me down, but it also makes me lose sight of my parents.

I wait for Dad to come back for me. "Let's go, Milo. Keep moving."

We find the ramp and take it to the field. Mom leads us toward the middle, and we settle onto the grass. As soon as we sit on the blanket we brought from home, my stomach growls. I'm hungry for the first time all day.

I'm halfway through my turkey sandwich when Mom hands me a Coke from our cooler. If Allie, my older sister, were here, she would definitely make some comment about how soda is terrible for me and how unfair it is that I get to drink it when *she* never did. Mom would shrug and say, "He's the second kid, and we're much older now. We pick our battles."

Allie now uses those same rules she grew up with to parent Jesse, who also happens to be my same age and my best friend—even though technically I'm his uncle because my parents are his grandparents.

On the field, our antennae bend in the breeze. It's super windy down here, and it brings whiffs of the stadium food: salty barbecue and sweet funnel cakes. But there's a sour smell too. It makes me glad that we brought our own lunch.

"This is actually going to happen," I tell my parents.

"Of course it is," Dad says.

Mom winks at me.

My nervousness produces energy. I can feel it in all six of my (real and fake) arms and legs. The realization of a lifelong dream when we—my mom, my dad, and I, along with two thousand plus of our insect-clad companions—will earn a world record.

I hold my phone above my head and take a picture of the crowd. I send it to Jesse with the hashtags #Guinness #greatness #recordsettingpests #worldrecord #myswarm.

"I'm ready to get this show on the road," Dad says. He rolls his shoulders. "This exoskeleton is super uncomfortable."

Mom shrugs. "Well, you didn't have to wear it during the drive. Plus, you should have made your costume with cardboard like mine. I feel fine."

"Plastic is definitely the better option. Yours doesn't have the right amount of sheen. Roach wings need to sparkle a little."

Our wings may sparkle, but they also lack airflow. I'm about to tell him this, but that's when it happens: the Smell.

Someone must have really let one rip. The odor is truly impressive... and disgusting. I hold my breath and wait for it to pass. When I venture to use my lungs again, the stink cloud barely lingers.

I'm all antsy and can't sit still. "I'll be right back," I tell my parents as I grab all our trash. The first two garbage cans are full, but I remember seeing one by the ramp. When I find it again, it's already in use. A dude has his arms draped over the top rim and his head is over the middle. His entire body tenses. I glance away too late and accidentally glimpse the hurlage. I cover my mouth to stop a sympathy gag.

I end up walking around the entire perimeter of the field before I find a trash can that isn't completely full.

When I rejoin my parents on the forty-yard line, Mom says, "That took you a while. You okay?"

"Yup. Just had to take the long way around."

Mom shrugs. "Sometimes that's the best way to get where you're going."

The Smell hits me again.

It's even stronger this time.

And disgusting—like a cross between a fart, skunk spray, and rotten milk.

Then I wonder, *Is it me?*

I check the bottom of my shoes first. Just dirt, no poop or anything. I do a quick check to make sure nobody's watching, and I tip my head down to sniff inside my bug body.

Smells fine-ish. As good as a plastic bug body can.

I tilt my head to one side and then the other. Not my armpits either.

Ugh. It's getting worse.

Mom and Dad have *got* to smell it too. The air is morphing into solid stinkness.

But my parents are acting normal—normal for them, at least. Dad rubs his hands together like something big and exciting is happening. Mom's lips pucker like she's part platypus; it's her Concentration Face. She's totally focused on the stage and the guy in the official blue blazer. He's the adjudicator who will tell us when we've broken the record and present the official certificate.

"We're getting the last folks registered," the adjudicator says into the sound system. "Once they're inside the stadium, we'll make this record thing official!"

We are *so* close. This is really happening!

As long as we don't all pass out first.

"Dad, do you smell that?"

"Huh?"

I make the official gesture of stink by waving my hand in front of my nose.

Dad sniffs and makes a face. "Nice one, Milo."

Mom says, "Do you need to use the bathroom?" She glances at her watch. "I think you'll have time, but you'll have to hurry."

"It's not *me*."

From the stage the adjudicator says, "Shouldn't be long now. And it's a good thing too. It's getting ripe in here. Whew!" He tugs at his collar. It's hard to tell when he's so far away, but I think he sways.

No, he's not swaying. It's all okay, I tell myself. *It's just in my head. Nerves or something.*

Still, the Smell grows—faster than my odor-acclimating skills can handle. And from the way people start to move and murmur, I know I'm not the only one who's noticed. All around me noses wrinkle. A lady just a few feet away dry heaves. I tell my own stomach and sympathy-gag reflex to simmer down.

"Whoa," the adjudicator says. He puts his palm to his forehead and wobbles. "Excuse me. I think—" But he never finishes his sentence. He puts his fist to his mouth and runs off the stage.

This finally gets Mom's attention. Her lips retract to their normal position. "What's going on?"

If she has to ask, something is *seriously* wrong with her nose.

"The smell." Dad sniffs the air like a dog tracking a scent.

"Is it a gas leak?" I ask.

He sniffs again. "Maybe. I think it's sewage related."

Mom shakes her head. "I barely smell anything."

Then we hear it: the unmistakable sound of somebody retching. Loudly. It's coming out of the stadium speakers. The volume is so loud and clear, we can even hear the splatter as it hits the ground.

The murmurs of the crowd die down. More than two thousand people get quiet, listening with heads tilted.

There's a groan, and it happens again.

"Turn off your mic!" somebody yells, and I start to understand. We're listening to the adjudicator get sick in surround sound.

We all stand there like we have no idea what to do. Until, in the distance, somebody else pukes.

"Excuse me," says a lady with butterfly wings. She pushes through the crowd, elbowing people out of the way—I take a hit in the upper arm—as she makes a path to the exit.

A guy in a spider costume runs by. He's got one hand over his mouth and the other over his backside.

Dad watches him pass. "That seems unpleasant."

Then the field is like an anthill that somebody stepped

on. Total chaos. People run toward the exit ramps. Everybody's pushing because they can't get through. Bug costumes are stripped and left behind.

"Where are they going?" Dad asks and frowns.

"I need to be first," a guy yells. "I'm gonna go in my pants!"

A lady with her arms wrapped around her stomach shakes her head. "Just let it happen. There's no stopping it."

"No!" the guy screams. He turns and runs in the opposite direction.

"We were poisoned!" says a shirtless guy with his chest and extra-large stomach painted in yellow and black stripes like a bee. The paint's rubbed off around his belly button. "It was the food! We're all going down!"

"Will we break the record if they all leave?" Mom asks.

"Surely," Dad says. "Let's just wait this out."

Mom, Dad, and I stand in the middle of the field with our sack lunch staying firmly in our stomachs.

There is a record set at the stadium in Abilene that day: THE MOST FOOD POISONING VICTIMS ever recorded at a single place—the puking adjudicator verifies it.

Except my family and I are bystanders. We are an audience of three, watching everybody else reach our goal without us.

I wish I'd run to a trash can and taken a bite of somebody's leftovers. Just a tiny nibble.

CHAPTER 4

We wait for the crowd to clear before we leave the stadium. We stepped in so many unidentified puddles on the way to the car, Mom tells us to peel off our sneakers. She holds them out the window by the laces until we find a place to dump them.

We're headed back to the hotel when Mom says, "You know, since we finished early, maybe we should skip the hotel and head home."

"No," I say too fast. I try to fix it by adding, "We could stop by Redbud Park and see where Cole Patterson set the world record for most consecutive bunny hops on a unicycle."

"If Cole Patterson were there," Mom says, "I'd agree with you. But since he's not, head east, please, sir." Mom puts our address in the GPS.

I sit back in my seat and cross my arms. "I want to see the park." I know I sound like I'm whining. But that's just because I am.

"Milo," Mom says. "We're not even wearing shoes."

"Not a problem." I lean up between their seats. "We can go buy some."

The GPS says to turn left. Dad listens and says, "Sorry, Milo. I just do what I'm told."

We usually take our time driving back from these trips—actually, we usually take *too* much time. We stop anytime a billboard suggests. We've pulled over for the World's Largest Peanut in Texas, multiple Billy the Kid memorials in New Mexico, and so many wax museums that I don't know how any supplies are left to make candles.

But, of course, now that I don't want to be home, we're barreling down the road.

The thing is, I told everybody at school I'd come back with a win.

Plus, Jesse keeps texting me. He wants a play-by-play of the record breaking.

At first, I ignore his questions, but when he texts: Did you get the record? I almost send: for epic diarrhea. Instead, I text back: A record was most definitely set.

I can already picture what will happen as I walk into school tomorrow:

Jesse will hold out his hand for a high five, but I'll know I don't deserve it. I'll sag my shoulders and shake my head and shuffle to class, hoping nobody notices me.

"There he is," someone will shout. "The Guinness Guy!"

I'll try to think of something funny to say so I don't look like such a loser, but I'll fail.

They'll say, "Hey, you don't look like a guy who just achieved the ultimate goal."

I'll say, "I'm not."

They'll say, "Whoa. That's really lame." Or "embarrassing" or "devastating" or, worse, "*expected*." Then the teacher will tell everybody to sit down and stop picking on the nobody.

But I refuse to think about that now.

Tomorrow I'll confess that my defining moment went terribly wrong.

CHAPTER 5

This morning I hit my snooze button three times and I don't have time to shower. I lean under the faucet and wet my hair.

When I come downstairs, Mom has a piece of toast in her mouth as she rushes around the kitchen. Dad says he'll drop me off at school on his way to work.

When he pulls up to the school, he scribbles an absence-excuse note using the console as a table. He hands me the note, and I bail out of the car and run up the steps of the school. My plan is to drop off the note, run to my locker, then hightail it to class. But as soon as I'm through the doors, the last bell rings. Now I need a tardy slip too.

Mr. Amondo, the principal, has already started the morning announcements when I stop by the office. I add my absence excuse to the tray and wait for Mrs. Grady, the lady at the front desk, to write me a tardy slip.

Before she hands it to me though, Mr. Amondo steps away from the microphone during the moment of silence and looks at the note I just put in the tray. "Ah, you're Mr. Moss. Stay here and we'll go to my office for a little chat." Before I can respond, he's back on the school-wide intercom reminding us about "displaying proper lunchroom behavior."

"Follow me," Mr. Amondo says once the announcements are finished.

I follow him through the hallway and into his office. He points to a chair in front of his desk. I sit and put my backpack at my feet.

The principal takes his time straightening the pencil holder, the stapler, and a Principal of the Year plaque from 2016. He clears his throat and adjusts the stapler one more time.

"So," he finally says, putting his elbows on the desk and leaning forward. "How's seventh grade so far? I know it can be a lot. You kids go from being the big man on campus to the youngest in the span of a summer. Plus, there's more responsibility, the stakes are higher, and there's a lot of new people."

"I think it's good so far."

Mr. Amondo smiles like I've answered correctly. I relax a little.

"And do you find that the work, the concepts are more…difficult?"

This question feels like a trick. Like it will end with either tutoring or more work. Playing it safe, I go with "Sometimes."

Mr. Amondo opens a folder on his desk and slowly drags his finger down the page inside. I wonder if there is anything he's looking for, or if it is just a prop to make students nervous. If so, it works.

"I wanted to talk to you because your name has recently come across my desk in one of the attendance reports. Are you aware that you've already missed six days this year?" He raises his eyebrows. "And we've only been back in school for a month."

I swallow. "Um, yes, sir?"

Mr. Amondo frowns. "Milo, do you know what 'at risk' means?"

Ummm. I know those words. So I say, "Sort of?"

"It's a term we use to describe students who are *at risk*"—he uses air quotes—"of having trouble in school."

"Okay," I say because there's not really a good response. I mean, *Cool* or *Stinks for them* doesn't feel appropriate.

"And did you know"—he leans forward again—"that missing school can put kids *at risk*?"

"No, sir," I say.

He consults the paper again. "You're in middle school now. What you do matters. Your actions and decisions will have lasting consequences."

"Um. Yes, sir. But I've done all the makeup work."

Mr. Amondo sighs and leans back in his chair. "That many absences can turn into a problem. Do you get me?"

No. "Yes, sir." My leg wants to shake so badly. I press my hand to my knee to hold it down.

Mr. Amondo smiles—or maybe grimaces—I can't tell. "So from now I'll count on you not to miss any more school. Okay?"

"Yes, sir."

"Perfect." He straightens the already-straight papers on his desk. He glances at his watch, sighs, and then scribbles something on a pink pad of paper. "Here. Give this to your teacher. And hurry. You don't want to miss anything. Don't forget what we talked about. It's important we do well, that we prove ourselves."

"Yes, sir. Thank you. I understand."

I stand up and yank my too-heavy backpack onto my shoulder.

CHAPTER 6

The hallways are completely empty now. My footsteps are too loud and echoey.

At my locker, I pull my binder out of my backpack and shove the bag into my locker. As I walk by open doorways, heads turn in my direction. Finally, I make it to Mrs. Docet's math class and stumble inside. It takes less than a second to know that something is not right.

At first, I think I'm in the wrong class, but then I spot Jesse. He's not in his normal chair. Okay, so...right room, wrong seats.

I go to Mrs. Docet's desk and put the pass on the corner of it.

"Get to work," she says.

"Yes, ma'am," I answer. "Except—"

"Except *what*?" she snaps.

"Somebody is in my seat."

"Read the board!" She points behind her. On the whiteboard, in big, sloppy handwriting, it says: *Find ONE partner and complete page 47. Your teacher has a MIGRAINE. Unless you want DETENTION, do your work and WHISPER!*

She uses her hand to shield her eyes from the light. "Who doesn't have a partner?"

Nobody answers.

She sighs, puts both hands on her desk, and stands slowly. "I know there was an odd number earlier." She closes her eyes and rubs her temples. "So. *Who* doesn't have a *partner?*"

"Me," somebody says. "But I'd rather do this alone."

It is Brandon Rosten. My nemesis.

Nope. We definitely cannot be partners.

"Alone works for me too," I add.

Mrs. Docet stops massaging her head to glare at us. "*Not* an option."

"If Brandon doesn't want a partner, Milo can work with us." Good old Jesse trying to save me.

Mrs. Docet's face relaxes into a gentle smile. It's the same expression all adults get whenever they talk to him. "Thank you, Jesse. That's very nice, but not today." Then her eyes narrow again as she refocuses her scowl in my direction. "Milo and Brandon are partners. If that is not ideal, maybe next time Mr. Moss will be on time." To the whiteboard she adds: *Do NOT argue with me or you will go to the PRINCIPAL!!!* She puts the dots on her exclamation points with unnecessary force.

Since I'm not ready to double my previous principal-visiting tally, I make my way back to my "partner" and sit in the desk next to his.

"Great," Mrs. Docet says. "Now work." She eases into her chair, leans back, and closes her eyes.

So this is happening. Brandon is my partner.

I glance up and Jesse's watching me. We have a silent conversation across the classroom.

Him: super-wide eyes. (Translation: *I'm soooo sorry you have to partner up with him.*)

Me: slight nod followed by a shrug of the shoulders. (Translation: *Right?*)

Him: extreme eye roll. (Translation: *Gah! Brandon is such a jerk.*)

Me: raised eyebrows and nodding. (Translation: *He is. I don't deserve this punishment.*)

But I can do it. I can work with him. I'm not the unreasonable one. "How do you want to do this?" I ask.

Brandon answers, "Alone."

I roll my eyes and glance at his paper. "You've already done number one. You take the odds and I'll take the evens?"

"No," he says.

Okay. I check the clock. There's zero chance we can get through this assignment if we don't do this together. Since my *partner* isn't going to help me, I decide to start on the last question of the assignment and work my way up. At the end of class, when he's not finished, we can staple our halves together. Win-win. We don't have to interact, and the assignment gets done.

I write down number thirteen on my paper. But here's the problem: Every question gets harder, so the last one is the most difficult. I don't get it at all. In the book, I flip to the front of the lesson and skim through the definitions and examples. I finish reading and check the time again. Of course, the minute hand moves too fast.

I have no option—I must poke the beast.

"Can I see how you did the first couple?"

Brandon pulls his notebook closer toward himself. "No."

I breathe deeply. I *can* be nice to him. I *will* be nice to him. "We're running out of time. You can take credit for all my work; I just need to understand it first. There's no way we'll finish otherwise."

He tips his head to the side as he considers this. He says, "Nope. I'll finish. You won't."

"We're supposed to work together."

He sits up straighter, panic tightening his face. "Oh no!" he says. Then his wide eyes narrow to slits. "Oh wait... still don't care."

It doesn't take much to be the bigger person.

If Brandon won't help, I'll just do it myself.

As I'm solving the first question *on my own*, I mumble, "If there was a record for biggest jerk, you'd win."

He either doesn't hear me or doesn't care.

"Ten minutes," Mrs. Docet says, still not opening her eyes.

I've only finished number one, thirteen, and twelve—and the last two are probably wrong—when Mrs. Docet says, "Turn your papers in. Get ready to go. And stay *quiet*."

I want to throw my pencil. Specifically, I want to throw it at Brandon.

"We're not done," I say.

"I am."

I'm forced to break the whiteboard rules and approach my teacher's desk. "Can I turn this in tomorrow?" I ask Mrs. Docet. "I didn't finish. I didn't understand it."

She snatches my paper like she doesn't believe me, then she studies the board like she's seeing if it breaks any of her migraine rules. "Your partner should have explained it."

"Oh, um." I try to come up with a good excuse. Or at least a respectful way to explain that my partner wouldn't spit on me if I burst into flames. Instead, I just go with "He didn't."

Mrs. Docet slaps my paper on her desk. "Brandon," she snaps. "Here. *Now.*"

Brandon trudges up the aisle. He gives me one last I-can't-stand-you glare and then fixes his face before he talks to the teacher. "Yeah?"

Mrs. Docet's voice sounds overly sweet as she says, "Can you explain why you didn't feel the need to do what I asked?"

"I did it on my own," he says.

"And tell me about how you worked with your partner. You *did* do that, right?"

"No, but—"

"So do you and your partner have something to turn in? Or were you lying?"

"No, ma'am." Brandon's jaw clenches and unclenches. "I mean, yes, we do."

Mrs. Docet holds out her hand. "Let me see it."

Brandon gets his paper from the basket, and I give her mine—which is really more of a blank page with a bunch of eraser marks on it. She studies both and then staples them together. "The highest grade you can get is a fifty since you are turning in only half of the assignment."

"But I did it all," Brandon says.

"And that's why you aren't getting a zero. Because I'm accepting half of your work and half of your partner's. Now"—she puts her hands on her hair like she's trying to keep her head attached—"both of you can go to your seats."

As soon as the bell rings, Jesse's at my desk. "I had no idea you were back, or I would have saved you. Dude, I'm so sorry."

"It's fine," I tell him as we walk into the hallway. Funny—I wasn't mad at him at all before, but now that he's taken the blame, I sort of am.

"So," he says as we walk through the hallway. "How does it feel to be a Guinness World Record holder?"

Before I can answer, Jesse stops in the hallway and points at me.

"This guy!" he yells. "Right here! Your children will be talking about him for generations to come."

People don't stop, but they do slow down to watch us. Or, at least, they watch Jesse. He may be short, but he's got a huge mouth.

"Quit it." I push his hand down. "Don't make this a big deal."

He responds by yelling, "A local treasure!"

"Stop!"

"Sorry, man," he says. "I'm just super proud of my uncle."

CHAPTER 7

Second period is social studies. This is my best subject thanks to Guinness, since the records can be set anywhere by anybody. Like the record for the HEAVIEST WEIGHT PULLED BY EYE SOCKETS was set in Italy but by a dude from Australia. I know about Zimbabwe, since it's the location of seven different records. I even know where to find Holy See, the SMALLEST COUNTRY IN THE WORLD, on the map.

Today we're in the library to do research for a project. We're supposed to create our own country—which doesn't sound awful at first, but it is Mrs. Pham's way of making us research, like, everything. We have to choose the government, the land, the animals that live there, and the things our country makes. So I'm the king of a small island with record-setting kangaroos. But I don't know what we export yet. We have to present everything to the class next Wednesday.

I still need to check up on the feeding habits of my kangaroo clan so I know what crops to grow, but Brandon is camped out in the nonfiction part of the library. I know after math, revenge is inevitable, but I'm not going to make it easy for him.

Whatever. I need to work on my slides for the presentation part anyway. For extra safety, I sit at the computer closest to Mrs. Moore, the librarian. I'm not scared or anything, but maintaining the nemesis/nemeset relationship means you never leave yourself exposed.

I'm making my third slide when I hear Brandon say, "I need to get my Google account information." He's at the librarian's desk.

I stare at my computer screen. Mrs. Moore plops the huge binder in front of him. "You should really know your log-in stuff by now," she tells Brandon. "It's just your first and last initial and ID number."

"Yes, ma'am," he says. "I'll write it down so I won't

forget. Thanks, Mrs. Moore." He closes the binder. "You've really helped me get what I need."

I swear I can feel his glare. I only let myself glance up when I know he's walking away. He heads back toward the nonfiction section as he slides a folded piece of paper in his back pocket.

I wonder if you can train kangaroos to attack.

CHAPTER 8

According to Guinness, there's a lady named Kim Goodman who can make her eyeballs go a half inch past their sockets. It's like she has real live googly eyes. She holds the record for FARTHEST EYEBALL POP.

I'm pretty sure I could compete with her when we're at lunch and Jesse says, "Did you bring the Guinness certificate? Can we see it?"

"Nah," I say, and force a shrug.

"That's okay," Jesse says. "You can show me after school."

I have two choices right now: come clean or double down.

We're sitting at the table with two people who went to our elementary school—Jason and Kyle—and three people that didn't—Justin, Darius, and Luke.

"This guy," Jesse announces to everybody at the table, "has been trying to break into Guinness since birth."

"Yeah, well," I start to say, but then Mr. Amondo's words come back to me: What I do now matters. I don't want to be known as the kid who has always *tried* to break a record. I want to be known as the kid who did it. "Lifelong goals typically take a while."

"Cool," Darius says. "Which record did you break?"

"Oh, just this group-participation thing."

"They were all dressed as rodents," Jesse adds.

"Insects," I correct. "We were all dressed as insects."

"That's…weird," Luke says.

Jason shakes his head. "Not if it gets you a record."

Luke wrinkles his nose. "I guess."

Jesse leans toward me. "Don't look behind you, Milo. Brandon's coming."

I catch sight of him in my peripheral vision, and not just because he is big. Big as in tall. And big as in if we ever got in an actual fistfight, I'd spend a significant amount of time picking up my teeth from the floor.

As Brandon walks by, Jason says to the table, "Milo and Brandon can't *stand* each other."

"Thanks for the awkwardness," I say after I'm sure Brandon has passed us.

"What's the story there?" Luke asks.

I shrug. "It's just how it's always been."

But that's not really true. Our rivalry officially started five years ago, in second grade. Jesse, Brandon, and I were in the same class. Amy Edgekin's mom brought holiday treats—cupcakes with green and red frosting, and they each had a plastic ring with a shiny, raised outline of a reindeer.

I don't remember who did it first, but somebody showed us if you scribbled an ink spot on your paper and then pressed your ring in it, the raised part would pick up the color and—*voilà!*—you had a stamp.

It was genius!

We all had a trail of stamps on our arms and faces before Mrs. Holmes caught us. It took, like, a half hour and three packages of baby wipes to erase our masterpieces—except Henry Phillips's stamps stayed on because he'd managed to get ahold of a Sharpie.

At the end of the day, we were allowed to get our

rings out of our desks. Around the same time, Jesse walked back into the room. Back then he spent the last twenty minutes of school in the counselor's office. When Jesse reached in his desk for the ring, it was missing.

We scoured the entire classroom. The garbage led us to our first clue: a broken ring. *But* it was not Jesse's, because the one we found had an orange tint and Jesse had used a blue marker.

When the final bell rang, our teacher made us stay. Jesse was sobbing.

Then I noticed Brandon's guilty expression and his pink cheeks. Plus, he was the only one not searching. He was definitely the thief.

"Brandon took it!" I said.

"Milo, we can't start accusing people," my teacher said. "I'm sure the ring will turn up. Jesse probably just misplaced it."

Mrs. Holmes gave up and let us leave. Brandon never admitted he took it.

I had to listen to Jesse's shuddering breaths all the way home. The inside of his left nostril was shiny from snot. I gave him my ring and said, "Don't worry. I'll take care of this."

I kept my promise. The next time we played dodge-ball, I made sure Brandon was the first one out. The day after that, Brandon told everybody if I wasn't picked last for one of the teams in PE, whoever called my name would be sorry. The next month, I "forgot" to give Brandon a valentine even though we were required to give them to the entire class. Our rivalry only grew from there. Maybe other things are changing, but at least I can count on my feud with Brandon to continue in middle school.

CHAPTER 9

A guy named Ananta Ram KC from Nepal holds the record for the LONGEST SPEECH MARATHON. He talked for over ninety hours. Somehow Jesse's incessant chatter feels longer than that as we walk to my house.

"I smoked Brandon in cross-country today for messing with you."

"Jesse, you always smoke everybody in cross-country."

Jesse got his endurance from Allie, who got it from both of my parents. But apparently I didn't get those genetics. Jesse has the same green eyes as our side of the family too, though he's got the darker skin of his dad. He's strong like Todd was too. Basically Jesse is the worst person to constantly be compared to—which happens when you are related and the same age. It's even worse when people find out that I'm his uncle. All I've got to beat Jesse is my height, but I'm average so I'm sure he'll pass me up soon.

"Yeah, but today I did it on purpose." He pats me on the back. "So, do you think you guys will stop the attempts now?"

Would we stop if we broke a record? I guess I don't know the answer. "I don't think so."

"Yeah. Can't imagine what Nina and Pops would do without them."

Jesse is used to all the record stuff. When my parents make a gigantic, almost-record-setting flan, Jesse grabs a spoon and digs in. When he's searching for a pencil and finds three drawers full of dice, he mentally files that info away for the next time we play Farkle. When the Toilet Paper Tower in the kitchen threatens to tip, Jesse knows how to help right it. It's convenient, really, to have a family member double as your best friend.

"So," I say, changing the subject. "When's the last time you washed your gym clothes?"

Jesse smiles and lifts his arm. "Take a whiff. What you're smelling is victory."

Every day, Jesse and I come to my house right after school. Our routine is eating Fruity Pebbles, doing homework, and playing video games—even though they lost their appeal for me after Mom, Dad, and I played *Fortnite* for hours to break a record. We were a mere sixty-seven minutes short of victory when a storm knocked out our electricity.

We've put our bowls in the sink and have barely started our homework when Mom walks into the kitchen. She has her own branding business and works from home, so she's here most of the time after school. She kisses us both on the heads.

"Working hard or hardly working?" Dad asks as he comes in from the garage.

"Dad. When you say the same joke every day, it's not funny."

He pats me on the shoulder. "It's an old joke, but it's a classic. Classics should be admired, never retired."

"*Anyways*," Mom says. "How was school?" Before we can answer, she adds, "Hold that thought." She eyes the Toilet Paper Tower that lives between the kitchen table and the back wall. "This thing is creeping again. Will you guys help?"

Mom puts her back to the stacked toilet paper rolls, squats into a wall-sit position, and pushes against it. The top of the Tower wobbles. I rush over to steady it before the whole thing collapses. Jesse and Dad brace the sides.

It's a mystery how the Toilet Paper Tower migrates. Mom's theory is it absorbs the humidity and swells; Dad thinks the foundation of our house must be slightly angled; Jesse and I have a complicated story involving aliens and nasal probing.

We don't have to know how it happens to be invested in keeping the TP Tower straight. We've all seen what happens if it falls. The rolls go everywhere. Half of them unwind. It takes us forever to wrap them back up, and we can never get the TP as tight as it started—the loose rolls create an increasingly unstable structure. Plus, when you grab a hand-spun roll in your moment of need, it's unsettling to know somebody has pre-handled the toilet paper.

Though the Tower problem should be self-righting as the pile gets smaller, it's not. Anytime my parents find a good deal on toilet paper, they buy as much as they can. The pile's actually *growing*.

"Thanks, boys." Mom steps back to look at it. "The humidity must be high today."

Dad nods. "Maybe if it rains tonight, it will expand so much that it'll fill up the house while we're sleeping. The headline in the papers will read, 'Choked by Charmin.'" Except he doesn't say "Charmin" the right way because he makes it start with the same sound as "choked."

When I point this out, he says, "Yeah, but that's not as catchy. We'll pronounce it 'ch' for the sake of the article."

I know he's kidding. I think he's kidding. But, the thing is, sometimes he's not.

In case he's serious, I say, "Nobody will know they're supposed to pronounce it that way."

"We'll use an asterisk to explain it."

Mom cuts off the discussion. "We stopped work early for an attempt. You boys want to join us?"

"So you're going for another record, huh?"

"What's the attempt?" I ask before Jesse can say anything else, worried my cover is about to be blown.

"Jumping through skimpies," Dad says.

"Skimpies?" Jesse asks.

"Underwear," Mom says.

"Nah." I shake my head. "We've got too much homework to do the record stuff right now."

Dad nods. "You do what you've got to do. But we'll save a pair of tighty-whities for you."

"I guess that's our answer, then," Jesse says to me after they leave. "You guys will still try to break records." He almost seems sad about it.

Somewhere in the background, my mom yells, "GO!"

My chest feels too tight; my stomach hurts.

Jesse and I don't lie to each other. Although, in fairness, he wouldn't ever need to lie. He does everything right. If he were me, he'd already have ten records broken by now.

But that isn't an excuse. Jesse is my best friend. He's family. I need to tell him the truth.

I open by mouth to confess, but in the background Mom yells, "STOP!" Even though I know she's not talking to me, I listen.

Before I say another word, there is a sudden *CRASH* and the unmistakable sound of shattering glass.

CHAPTER 10

Jesse and I freeze. He stares at me with wide eyes. I hold my breath.

From the other room, I hear Mom ask, "Are you okay?" in her something-is-wrong voice.

Nobody answers.

Then there's crying. Very loud, very high-pitched crying.

Jesse and I shoot up, abandoning our homework. We run to the living room. The scene is worse than I imagined.

Dad's sitting in the middle of the coffee table. Seriously *in* it. Like, *inside* of it. He's folded in half like a taco; his feet are in the air, and his butt is on the ground. A million pieces of broken glass surround him. His head is tipped back, and his mouth is open wide. I'm not sure if he's even breathing.

Mom is on her knees, bent forward at the waist and holding her stomach.

She's sobbing.

But then, she snorts.

Yes. *Snorts*.

She's not actually crying. She's laughing. So hard, tears stream down her cheeks. Her face is all pinched up. Except for a couple of spontaneous pig noises, no other sounds come out.

Dad gasps.

So, good to know, he's not dying. He's just hysterically laughing too.

I notice a new detail in this scene. Dad has neon green underwear over his pants. As in, he is wearing underwear on the outside of his clothes.

He puts an arm on each side of the coffee table frame and pushes himself up, unfolding as he tries to stand.

He's successful—but only for a moment, then he steps away from the mess before he falls to his knees like Mom. He gasps, laughs, then gasps again.

Yup. That's definitely underwear over his khaki pants.

"Oh," Mom says, wiping her face with her hand. "Oh, gosh. That entire thing was recorded." My parents both lose it again.

The hysteria spreads. Now Jesse is laughing too.

It *is* pretty funny. To see Dad folded in the table. Until I notice the blood.

"I think you're hurt."

Dad turns his arm so he can see the back of it. "Ha! Look at that! You're right! I'm bleeding!" Then he guffaws. "And it's deep." Ha-ha-ha. "I need stitches."

Jesse's no longer smiling after glimpsing Dad's gash. "Should I, um, help or something?"

"Oh, honey," Mom says, finally catching her breath. "He's fine. Really. You're pale. You need to sit."

Jesse nods and obeys, lowering himself onto the couch. He always acts like this when there's blood. Even a drop.

"Milo. Could you get something for us? Like paper towels or a dishcloth?"

I listen, glad to leave, even just for a second. In the kitchen, I grab a roll of paper towels for Dad and a puke pitcher for Jesse.

"Thanks, honey," Mom says when I come back.

"Why don't you take Jesse...somewhere else?" We all know this is code for: *Get him out of here before he passes out.*

I help Jesse stand. He wobbles. I put his arm around my shoulders and lead him to my room. I tell him to sit on the bed, but he collapses into the desk chair, probably because it's the closest option.

"You need to breathe," I remind him.

He nods.

"You're going to be okay."

His eyes roll back so I see only the whites. He starts to tip. I catch him. "You need to sit on the bed. Or the floor," I say. It comes out harsher than I mean it, but I'm too busy trying to keep him from falling to worry about my tone.

He shakes his head like he's trying to wake himself up. "I'm fine," he says. "I'm okay."

"No, you aren't." And to prove it, I add, "Did you see all that blood?"

It works. Jesse's pupils disappear again. He rocks. I let him tip; gravity takes over, and I control the speed of the fall.

After he's propped against the wall, I sit next to him. "Take this." I hand him the pitcher. "Just in case." He holds it under his chin in ready position.

Jesse's aversion to blood started after his dad died. We were in second grade when it happened. Todd worked as a fireman, but that isn't how he was killed. Todd was on his way to work, and he stopped to help a lady with a flat tire. The lady told us later she was so thankful because she had her three kids in the car and with the rain, she was afraid she'd be stranded there for hours. Todd had just finished when a truck on the highway swerved. The truck hit the lady's car and my brother-in-law. The kids and the lady were okay. Todd was not.

Now, in my room, I wait with Jesse until he gets control of his own body, until he refiles whatever deep-down thoughts he needs to put away.

CHAPTER 11

My parents are at the ER to get Dad's arm checked out. Allie comes to get Jesse and me. They live close enough that we could walk, but Jesse can barely stand, so my sister gets us on the way home from work.

Jesse's Thursday chores are garbage and laundry, but when we get to his room he climbs into the bottom bunk and curls up. He stares across the room at the poster of his namesake, Jesse Owens. Jesse's dad hung the poster in his room before Jesse was even born.

"You okay?"

"Yeah." His voice cracks.

"Scoot over," I tell him, and sit on the edge of his bed.

"My mom texted. They're at the ER now and about to see the doctor. She sent the video of what Dad was supposed to be doing. Wanna see? It'll cheer you up." I click the Play button before Jesse can answer. Guinness's suggested challenge of the day reloads on the screen.

The guy in the video holds his arms out and walks in a circle to show the underwear over his pants. The slow spin is a pretty standard way to start these types of challenges. This is the attempter's way of saying: *There're no tricks here; behold this perfectly normal pair of undies/pants/ other necessary equipment.*

When the guy faces the camera again, he pulls down the underwear and steps out of the them. I spot my father's first problem. Dad wore his work khakis. This guy has on tight pants, like the kind runners wear.

The second glaring difference is that Dad is an engineer who sits at a desk most of the day. This dude looks like his job is lifting weights, and he's never missed a day of work.

On the video, the tight-wearing, muscle-flexing guy holds the underwear up and says he's ready. There's a beep, and the guy goes for it, jumping with his knees high and in sync. Both his feet go through the leg holes at the same time, and when he lands, the underwear is in place. The guy then pulls them off and jumps again.

In the bottom right of the screen, a ticker marks every success. After the guy completes nine jumps his timer dings. Underwear halfway on, he stops and puts his hands on his head and bends over. Sweat drips from his now-shiny face.

Yeah. I can't believe Dad even tried to beat this guy.

"So," I say, "that was interesting. Right?"

Jesse nods, but he doesn't get up.

"Here." I give him my phone. "You can watch it again. I'll get your chores done."

★ ★ ★

My sister is sitting at the kitchen table and grading papers. When I walk through to go to the laundry room, she looks up. "Where's your nephew?"

"He's in his room."

She sets her pen down and leans back in her chair. Allie nods and swallows. "So what are you up to?"

I shrug. "Just getting water."

I go over to the cabinet, get a glass, and fill it up from the sink.

"You're going to the laundry room, aren't you?"

"No." I gulp the water.

"I've told you not to do his chores. How's he supposed to learn responsibility if you do all his stuff?" Allie winks at me.

"I don't do *all* his stuff. Usually we split it."

She pulls out the chair next to her. "Sit down. Chat with me. Want some coffee? Just made it." She lifts her mug.

I hold my hand out, and she gives me the cup, just like she has since I was five years old. I take a sip. It's so gross. I make my involuntary disgusted face, and a shiver runs through my body. But even if I could stop my reaction, I wouldn't.

Allie cracks up like always. "That never gets old." She looks at her watch. "Whoops. Don't tell Mom and Dad I gave you caffeine so late."

"They might ground you."

"Worse," she says. "Dad might lecture me when he comes over to fix my garage door." She nods toward Jesse's room. "He okay?"

"Yeah. Just the blood thing."

Allie nods. "Wonder if he'll ever get over that."

I bite my lips together and shrug. Todd's stuff is all around the house as if he still lives here. His jacket hangs on the hooks by the front door. His sunglasses are on the windowsill over the sink. And even though Mom came over and helped Allie pack up Todd's stuff when he died five years ago, I know all the boxes are still in the garage.

"Anyways," Allie says, picking up the stack of papers and standing. "Jesse's got swim practice in an hour. Would you mind passing on the message that he's got approximately forty-eight minutes to recover and to do his laundry?"

"Got it," I tell her. Then I finish the rest of his chores.

CHAPTER 12

After we drop Jesse off at swim, Allie takes me home.
"I thought I'd help you pick up the coffee table
guts before Mom and Dad get back," she says as she walks
up to the door.

Allie and I work together to clean up the mess. While
I lift the table frame out of the way, Allie uses the broom
to push the chunks of glass out from under it. Then she
holds the dustpan as I sweep the pieces into it.

When we're done, Allie sits on the couch and nods at
the old-school camera that is still on the tripod.

"Obviously we need to watch that."

"Obviously," I say, even though I don't want to.

Allie gets the camera, adjusts it so we can both see the screen, and presses Play.

We can't see Mom in the recording, but we can hear her narrating. "This is for the underwear jumping record. Johnny, wave to the camera." Dad, wearing neon underwear over his khaki pants, waves.

Allie laughs. "This is already terrible."

Mom continues, "Johnny is going to attempt to beat nine jumps in thirty seconds."

Dad gives a thumbs-up and then points at the camera. "This is for you, honey."

Mom leans in front of the view. Only half her face shows. "What a man. Stay back, ladies. This guy's all mine."

I roll my eyes. Allie nudges me with her elbow. "Oh, come on. It's cute."

"Ready, set," Mom says on the video. "Go!"

Dad definitely goes. He pulls down the underwear, steps out of them, and then jumps with both feet. He makes it through the leg holes and pulls the underwear up. Then down and then off. He jumps back in with both feet. Up, down, off again.

"Fifteen more seconds!" Mom calls out.

Dad's breathing so hard. He stumbles on the next jump. He looks ridiculous—nothing like the guy on the website. Still, I find myself leaning forward, silently rooting for him even though I know how this is going to end.

He makes another jump. Undies up, then down. He's slowing down, losing steam. His hops are now more like steps.

"Five more seconds! Keep going!"

Don't do it, I think, as if I can actually change the ending.

He makes his final jump. His left foot makes it through, but his right foot gets caught. He wobbles, corrects himself, and then finally gets his second leg through.

"Stop!" Mom calls.

That's it. It's over. He didn't fall.

For a second, hope is stronger than truth.

The challenge is over, but Dad is still off-balance. He takes one step back to keep from falling, then another step. And then it happens. His leg hits the edge of the coffee table, he sways and...I close my eyes for the inevitable.

Crash.

On the video, Jesse and I run into the room.

Mom's bent over cry-laughing. Dad's cracking up so

hard, he's making no sound. Jesse scrunches his face like he's trying to solve a puzzle, then he starts laughing too.

On the couch in real time, Allie is cracking up. She's practically convulsing.

There are some truly epic fails in the history of Guinness.

This one time in Iran, a group set out to beat the record for the WORLD'S LARGEST SANDWICH. They might have won—if the crowd hadn't gotten so hungry. The audience ate the sandwich before it was measured and recorded.

There was another guy who was going to break the record for fasting. To do this, he made a little glass box where people could watch him not eat. Only he forgot to tell Guinness he was attempting this challenge—and realized this after fifty days of starving.

What if those are our people? What if we never get a record no matter how many times we try? What if we never win? What if all I'm known for are my epic fails?

★ ★ ★

I get my laptop and sit back on the bed. I glance at the door even though I know nobody else is home, and I type "Guinness World Record Certificate" in the Google search bar and press Enter. When the results pop up on the screen, I click on the Images tab.

Scrolling through a couple of rows of pictures, I click on the certificate without a watermark and save it as a PDF file to my desktop. It's an outdated record for the LONGEST CROCHETED SCARF—TEAM set by Mother India's Crochet Queens in May 2017.

I whisper an apology to the Crochet Queens as I use a text box to cover the information about their record-setting 46,223-foot 9-inch scarf and type in, "The record for the largest crowd of people dressed as insects was achieved at Shotwell Stadium in Abilene, Texas." I save the newest version and print.

In the office, I grab the certificate off the printer and hurry back to my room. It looks legit—exactly like the one that should have been ours. It even has the "Officially Amazing" logo at the bottom. If I hadn't made the certificate myself, I would never know it was fake.

The garage door hums as it opens. My parents are home.

"Milo?" Dad calls out.

"Coming!" I slip the fake certificate into my backpack

and go downstairs. Mom is in the kitchen. She fills a mug with coffee.

"You're back. How's the arm?"

"As soon as we walked into the ER with those bloody paper towels, we got tons of attention." Mom laughs. "I think they were worried about us freaking everybody else out. The nurse took us straight to a room."

Dad holds up his arm, which is covered in white gauze from his fingers to his elbow. "Guess what! Twenty-seven stitches! Can you believe it? Doctor said it was lucky I didn't hit the artery, or I could have bled to death."

Picturing twenty-seven stitches under that wrap is enough to make me have a Jesse-type reaction. I hold on to the back of the chair. "Are you okay?"

"Mostly. Just bummed because this many stitches should be a record."

"Oh. Um. I'm sorry you weren't more hurt?"

"I searched the internet while he was getting sewn up," Mom says. "There's a lady named Denise Bartlett who holds a world record for two hundred ten."

"I wonder how many stiches Richard Browning got on his way to victory?" Dad says as we go to the living room.

"We may never know," says Mom.

"I may not have gotten *the* record for my stitches," Dad says, "but the doctor said I did get the most stitches of any patient *he's* had so far."

"That's right, honey," Mom says. "That victory is all yours."

CHAPTER 13

"Glad Pops is okay," Jesse says before the bell rings. I didn't get to talk to him in math, and we don't have second period together, but we're in the same class for third period, language arts, and fourth period, Computer.

"Yup. Twenty-seven stitches." I add, "It wasn't a record. And speaking of which..." I slip the fake Guinness certificate from my binder and hand it to Jesse.

"Cool!" he says, taking the paper from me. "Huh." He frowns. "They spelled *people* wrong."

"Let me see." I snatch the page back from him. Sure enough, "people" is spelled "peeple." I take a deep breath. "Yeah. Weird. I'll have to email about that."

Thankfully the teacher tells everybody to go to their seat. I cram the stupid certificate back into my binder. Dumb mistake. I'll print off a new one tonight.

"I need a volunteer to pass out papers," Mrs. Shafer says from the front of the room. Several kids raise their hands. She ignores them all. "Jesse, I absolutely loved your biography." She puts her hand to her chest. "Will you pass these out for me?"

"Huh?" Jesse says. He recovers quickly and takes the papers from the teacher.

It's official. Jesse has become her favorite. This means for our last assignment he must have used his go-to topic: his dad. Essay about a hero? Jesse's dad. Journal about a defining life moment? Jesse's dad. And, apparently, two-page narrative biography? Jesse's dad.

Now that Mrs. Shafer knows about Todd, it's only a matter of time before word spreads through the teachers' lounge. He'll be known as the brave young man who tragically lost his father. That's what Jesse was always known as in elementary school. It's just a bonus that he is good at everything else too.

As soon as Jesse finishes and sits down, Mrs. Shafer says, "Let me just say this is one of my favorite assignments to grade. I love finding out more about my students. Some of you really did well. Some of you did not." I swear she looks at me. I wrote about Richard Browning and his flight suit. I got a B.

Monica, the girl in the front row who asks a million questions, raises her hand.

"No questions yet," Mrs. Shafer says. "A narrative shouldn't read like a timeline on Wikipedia. You shouldn't just list the facts. You should show how the facts affect the person."

Monica raises her hand again. This time she waves it.

Mrs. Shafer holds up a finger. "I told you, hold your questions until I'm done."

Monica puts her arm down. She shifts in her seat.

"Flip through your pages and read the comments I made. These will be beneficial because we're going to give this another try. You need to show why a person's life events matter. How do they color the person's world? How do they change it?"

Monica raises her hand.

"Read the comments," Mrs. Shafer says.

"But if I don't go to the bathroom right now," Monica says, "I'm going to have a life event in my chair."

CHAPTER 14

It's Wednesday. Social studies presentation day.

I volunteer to go first, to get it out of the way. Otherwise I'll sit there and overthink and then stutter and *um* my way through. I get beat by Desiree. So now I have to go after the smartest, most know-it-all girl in the school. For her presentation, she wrote (and sang) her own national anthem and then passed out the national candy she invented, which is Flamin' Hot Cheetos covered with chocolate and caramel.

At least I can lower the bar for everybody else.

I plug the projector cord into my school computer and click the presentation icon. Mrs. Pham said we can have note cards, but when I grab mine, my adrenaline makes my fingers shake and my eyes can't focus on the words. I pretend I don't need them and toss the cards into the trash can at the front of the room.

I clear my throat and point to the first slide. I used an actual picture of Bishop Rock, but I stretched it out so it looks bigger. "All hail the king of Moss Rock."

Brandon laughs, but he's the only one. So I know he's not laughing with me—he's definitely laughing at me.

The next words fall out of my brain, and I can't remember what else I was going to say. I click to the next slide. There's a three-year-old picture of me in front of the castle at Disney World. My parents and I went there to see it because it has a record for TALLEST CASTLE INSIDE A THEME PARK. "In this monarchy, I'm the king."

I click to the next slide and show a field of alfalfa. "Here's the crop we grow. It has two purposes. One, it's our export. And, two..." I click to the next slide. "We grow the hay because our island is known for the record-setting boxing kangaroos."

Some kids laugh. A boy in the front row points at the slide and snorts. Even the teacher's smiling. I'm *nailing* this.

I glance back at the picture of the two kangaroos fighting.

Except this isn't the slide I put in there. In this picture there's only one kangaroo. It has a joey in its pouch. But the weird part is the big one has my old yearbook picture photoshopped on its face.

"That's not—"

I click to get the slide off the screen. But kangaroo-me doesn't go away. Instead, a small version of Jesse's face appears over the joey so it looks like I'm carrying him in the pouch.

Everybody is cracking up.

"I didn't do this!" I try to tell them.

And then I see him: Brandon sitting there all smug, with his arms crossed and a smirk on his stupid face. He winks at me.

That's it. He's getting it.

I stalk toward him. I've got approximately three seconds to figure out my next move. Punching him seems like a really good idea. I don't care that he's bigger than me, because I'm definitely madder. I clench my right hand into a fist.

"Milo. Stop. *Now.*" Mrs. Pham steps in the aisle to block me before I can get to Brandon's desk. Like she needs to protect him. Or maybe she's protecting me.

"In. The. Hall." Mrs. Pham points to the door.

I listen. The hallway's deserted and once I'm out of the classroom, my adrenaline fades. When I picture the kangaroo-me on the slide, my nose burns.

Mrs. Pham comes out a moment later. "I've called the principal to come get you."

"But *he* started it." I cringe because I just heard how dumb my words sound.

"He did nothing, and you accused him."

"But I—"

"Mr. Amondo," she says. "Thank you for coming."

"Yes." Mr. Amondo puts his hand on my shoulder. "Son, why don't you come with me and we can chat?"

Mrs. Pham crosses her arms. "When you come back to class, I expect you to treat my students with kindness and respect. I will not tolerate anything else."

She says this like Brandon is innocent, but she doesn't know he's been my bully since second grade. Stupid school with stupid teachers.

★ ★ ★

"*Mom?*" I say as soon as Allie answers the phone. "It's *me*, Milo."

"Did you call the wrong number? This is Allie."

"I'm in the principal's office."

"Milo?" She suddenly sounds out of breath. "What's wrong? Are you okay?"

"Yeah. I'm in trouble. I think. And they said I had to call a parent. So I called you."

I hear her take a deep breath.

"Ah, I see." She sounds like herself again. "I *do* suppose I'm a parent. Though did they specify it should be one of *your* parents?"

"No, ma'am."

"You must be in a lot of trouble. Okay, so tell me what you did, and I'll decide what we should do about it."

I tell her about the presentation. About *somebody* photoshopping my head on the kangaroo.

There's silence on the other end of the phone.

"Al—Mom?"

"Sorry." Her voice sounds strained. Like maybe she's crying... or laughing. "I'm here."

"But I promise I didn't do it."

Mr. Amondo crosses his arms.

"Though it *appears* that I am the only one with access to my account, and so it must have been me." I turn my head and whisper, "Except I saw Brandon look at the book with all our passcodes in the library."

The principal clears his throat.

"Well, as a mother," Allie says, "I am glad you didn't do this. Though as your sister, I'm a little disappointed you're not the one who made the picture." I can hear the smile in her voice. "So then you got in trouble for it?"

"Sort of. I got in trouble for yelling at the kid who did it."

Mr. Amondo holds his hand out for me to give him the phone.

I nod. "Umm, I think the principal wants to talk to you."

"Okay. I won't lie for you, but I'll see what I can do on one condition."

"What?"

"I'm going to need to see this picture. I think I need it for our Christmas card."

I should have called Mom or Dad.

"I'd rather have detention for life," I whisper, and then I hold out the phone.

"Hello, this is Mr. Amondo." He pauses. "Oh yes. I agree," he says. "Consequences are important." Another pause. "Well, I was just going to—" Mr. Amondo nods. "Okay. Yes. That sounds good. Yes. Thank you. Um, okay, I will do that." Then he hangs up the phone.

"So..." He turns back to me. "I was going to give you a lunch detention, but your mother seems to think you should have two days of after-school detention."

"What?"

He takes out a notepad and starts writing something. "So that's what we'll do." He rips off the top sheet and hands it to me. "Here's the pass for both days after school. She also asked me to tell you something."

"Okay?"

"She said to tell you that your sister loves you...? She said you'd understand."

"Yup." I nod. "Got it."

CHAPTER 15

After-school detention is in the life science room. I've never been in here before today. There are five different stations, and each has a sink and a stove and counter space jutting out to the side. I slide out one of the barstools at the counter closest to the back where there are three computers. Apparently everything I need to know about how to serve my punishment is on a poster in the front of the room.

Welcome to DETENTION
- Sign in.
- No talking.
- Do your homework.

- You may not go to the bathroom.
- Don't get detention again.

Today it's just me and some kid I've never seen. He writes the whole time and doesn't acknowledge me or the teacher at all. Overall, detention is boring but not too bad.

Jesse hangs out in the library to wait for me after school. "How was it?" he asks with wide eyes.

I side-eye him while we're walking. "Fine."

"You okay?"

"Jesse. It was detention, not torture."

When we get to my house, I'm the one to ask if Jesse wants to play video games. There's something about the possibility of being grounded from electronics that makes them feel new again.

We're playing Xbox when Dad gets home.

"Hey, Pops," Jesse says, without looking away from the TV screen.

Dad answers by robot-dancing badly. His button-down shirt untucks on one side.

I shake my head. "Please, stop."

He responds by switching to the Macarena—but his version is more like him slapping his own shoulders and wiggling.

"Dad. That's not how it goes. At all."

Jesse laughs, so Dad keeps going.

"Pops, can I ask you some questions?" Jesse asks. "It's for school."

"Of course." Dad stops. "Let me change, and then you can ask away."

Jesse makes it to the last seven players before somebody snipes him from behind.

I start a new game.

"What do you want to ask my dad?" My player gets out in the first thirty seconds.

Jesse takes the controller from me. "I'm writing about him for the narrative."

"What? You can't do that."

Jesse shrugs. "Mrs. Shafer said I could."

"But he's not your dad."

"I know. I already wrote about *him*."

"But *I'm* writing about my dad." This could be true. I haven't decided. "We can't have the same paper."

"It'll be fine," Jesse says.

Of course it will be fine for him now that he's the golden child.

"I took the liberty of conducting a quick Guinness search," Dad says as he walks back into the room in jeans and a T-shirt. "We can do a boring interview *or* there's a couple of records we could go for. To break the existing world record, we'd only have to talk for over thirty hours, one minute, and forty-five seconds."

"I need to interview you too," I say.

"Great! Do you have"—Dad looks down at his phone—"forty-two more friends that want to come as well? Because the record for the most interviews in twelve hours is currently forty-three. We could definitely break that one."

"Nah," I say. Two is too many already.

"Okay." Dad sits in one of the swivel chairs next to the couch. "I'm all yours."

Jesse turns off the game. He doesn't even offer to let me take over.

"Hold on." Jesse gets up and rifles through his backpack next to the front door. He slides out a sheet of paper covered in his handwriting. "I wrote down some questions I wanted to ask." He puts the paper on the side table and leans over to consult it. "So where did you grow up?"

"Let's start from the beginning," Dad says. "I was born in the middle of a snowstorm. In the mountains. On the side of the road."

I roll my eyes. "You were born in Texas in July."

"Do you want this to be true or interesting?"

Jesse laughs at Dad's dumb joke.

"We're actually not supposed to work on this together." I stand up. "I'll do my interview later."

"You sure?" Jesse asks.

"Yup."

I go to the kitchen and sit at the table to brainstorm my own list of questions. I can only think of stuff to ask that is either boring or that I already know.

I jot them down anyway: *Where were you born? Where did you grow up? Where did you go to college?*

I include the answers.

I'm pouring a glass of orange juice when I hear Mom in the living room too. She's talking about the *giant cake pan*.

This is bad.

This means they are talking about world records. Like the record I lied to Jesse about.

I abandon the juice and rush into the living room.

"Hey, honey," Mom says to me as I sit down on the couch.

I force a smile. "Why are you talking about the cake thing again? We all already know this story."

"We were reminiscing about how we started the record breaking," Dad says. "You've got to give the fans what they want. Now, where was I?" He looks up at the ceiling and scratches his chin.

Mom takes over. "So we were getting ready for your mom's wedding, Jesse. And, when I was researching, I found a post about the largest wedding cake ever. Fifteen thousand thirty two pounds."

"She talked about that record for weeks," Dad says. "So I surprised her, and I spent the entire day in the garage making a huge poorly welded cake pan. When I gave it to Nina, she bought all the cake mix within a thirty-mile radius."

Mom nods. "We mixed it all together—one bowl at a time and poured the batters into the giant pan. And then we realized there was no hope of getting it in the oven. It wouldn't even fit through the door of the house. So we tried cooking it over a fire."

"And, boys, do you know what we learned from that experience?" Dad pauses and then delivers the punch-line. "That giant cakes in poorly welded pans do not cook well over a fire."

"Do you think my parents would have used it if it

worked?" Jesse asks. "The cake?" He puts his pencil tip to his paper like he's going to write down an answer.

"Oh goodness, no. Allie used to be a bit high-strung before—" Mom shakes her head. "Well, before she realized there were more important things. She wanted everything perfect for the wedding." She smiles softly. "And it was."

"And the rest is history!" I add. "We all know what happens after that. Allie gets married. You try for more records."

"Any more questions?" Dad asks.

"I think we're done," I say.

Jesse narrows his eyes. "Yeah. I guess I'm done."

"Then I have a question for y'all." Dad leans forward with a serious expression. "Did you know...if your feet smell and your nose runs, then you're built upside down?"

"Dad. Your jokes. Please, stop."

"I think they're funny," Jesse says.

Of course he does.

CHAPTER 16

Jesse is too quiet on the way to school the next day.

"Are you okay?" I ask.

"Fine," he says.

After another block of silence I ask, "You sure you're good?"

"Great," he says.

"Cool, cool. Did you know a guy in Peru gave five thousand one hundred seventy-four hugs in eight hours?"

"Neat," Jesse says.

"Also, a guy in Zimbabwe kept a diary for ninety-one years."

Jesse nods.

"To make the largest serving of guacamole, it took over twenty-five thousand avocados."

He stays quiet.

"Are you really going to make me keep going? I can do this all day."

"I don't see why you got mad that I interviewed Pops."

I shrug. "I don't know."

"He's my family too, you know."

"I know."

We take a right turn. The crossing guard is up ahead.

"You beat me at everything," I finally admit. "You can't be the favorite kid for writing about my dad *and* get a better grade while doing it."

We wait at the corner until the crossing guard steps into the middle of the street and holds up a stop sign.

"I don't beat you at *everything*," Jesse says. "I don't have a world record."

Neither do I, I think.

"Whatever," I say.

★ ★ ★

Thursday in Computer is internet scavenger hunt day. This means we read articles on the Schoolside News website and answer the questions Mrs. Morrow gives us. We're allowed to help one another if we get stuck, and Jesse and I take full advantage of this.

On the way to my seat, I grab a handout from Mrs. Morrow's desk. I also get one for Jesse and set it next to his computer. Jesse gets there right before the bell rings.

I go to the tab for Schoolside News, click on the Current Events section, and check the first question on the handout: *What is Diwali and how is it celebrated?* I already know the answer to this because we have a party to celebrate Diwali at school every year, but I still copy the info from the article. On my paper, I write, "The Festival of Lights. Diwali gets its name from the row of clay lamps set outside homes to symbolize the inner light that protects from spiritual darkness."

I move on to question two: *What are cracks on the moon's surface called, and what do scientists think are causing them?*

"Hey, Milo," Jesse whispers. "Look at this. I found an article you might be interested in." A picture of Shotwell Stadium in Abilene, Texas, fills my screen.

Oh no. Please, no.

Jesse sits there just waiting. I glance around to make sure nobody's watching, and I read:

BAD BEEF IN TEXAS: A WORLD-RECORD-FOOD-POISONING INCIDENT

Reportedly 1,182 people in Abilene, Texas, simultaneously earned a world record—but not the one they were attempting. These record setters all experienced food poisoning, allegedly from the brisket served by the 4U BBQ food truck, and suffered severe stomach cramps, diarrhea, and nausea due to the food-borne illness. All victims were part of the Guinness-record-setting attempt of MOST PEOPLE DRESSED AS INSECTS. Although the attendees were forced to abandon their insect-clad, record-setting hopes after the symptoms began, most still earned a record: MOST FOOD POISONING VICTIMS EVER RECORDED AT A SINGLE PLACE. Paramedics treated several of these award winners at the scene. At least 274 people were taken to a nearby hospital, where they were treated and released. The owner of 4U BBQ declined to comment at this time, although he did confirm that his business is not operating until the investigation is complete.

"Nope." I hit the Power button of his monitor. His screen turns black.

"What do you mean, *nope*?" Jesse turns his monitor back on.

In my peripheral vision, I see Mrs. Morrow slowly stand. She walks over to us. "Is there a problem here, boys?" she asks.

Jesse's screen pings back to life.

"His computer shut off," I say.

Jesse side-eyes me. "Something was wrong. But I'm fixing it now."

Mrs. Morrow nods. "Okay. Let me know if it happens again, and I'll check it out."

"He will," I say.

Once the teacher is back at her desk, Jesse leans over. "You lied to me."

The picture of Shotwell Stadium remains in full view on his computer. I consider using my foot to yank the plug from the wall.

"I promise I'll explain. After class."

He frowns. I mimic his expression.

"Everything still okay, boys?" Mrs. Morrow asks.

"Yes, ma'am," I say to the teacher. *"Later."* I lean in to tell Jesse. "I promise."

"As long as you promise. Because since I just caught you lying, I *totally* trust everything you say."

CHAPTER 17

The WORLD'S HEAVIEST APPLE is about four pounds; the HEAVIEST PEAR is about six and a half pounds; the HEAVIEST MANGO is over seven and a half pounds. And it feels like I ate them all as a fruit salad.

"You can't tell anybody," I say to Jesse as soon as we're in the hallway.

"Is this why you didn't want me interviewing Pops? Because you thought I'd find out?"

"No! Maybe? I don't know."

"You lied to me."

"I know. I had to though."

Jesse stops by his locker and puts his books inside. I wait for him.

He starts walking again. "I get it, I guess."

"Really?"

"Yeah. I mean. I get jealous of the record stuff sometimes, but I wouldn't want anybody to know about a world record for"—he leans over and whispers—"*diarrhea*."

"Hold on." I grab Jesse's arm and pull him to the side. "Look. You can't say anything to anybody." I look him right in the eyes so he knows how serious I am. "Please." I'm borderline begging.

"I won't say anything. And when I do my paper on Pops, I'll mention the record stuff, but I won't say what he got a record for."

I shake my head. "No. You don't get it. We didn't break a record. At all."

Jesse's forehead furrows. "Wait. So you *lied* lied."

I can't look at him. His eyes narrow with disgust. Of course he's disgusted. Perfect Jesse would never lie. Why would he? There's no reason to when you're perfect.

"You're going to have to tell everybody. I'm not lying for you." He shivers like he's sick at the very thought.

I focus on my right shoe. The lace is untied. "Okay."

"Okay," Jesse says, and he starts to leave.

"Wait!" I stop him. "But not today, okay?"

Perfect Jesse crosses his arms. "It's not gonna get any easier."

"But let me be the one to tell people. Give me time—a week at the most. It's just—you know Brandon made me look like a fool in class. Let me recover from that first. This can't all happen at once." And I can't be known as *the liar*. That's worse than being a record-breaking failure.

He huffs. "I'm not lying for you," he says again.

"I promise. You won't have to."

As soon as we get inside the cafeteria, Jesse splits from me to go through the lunch line.

I go to our usual table. Jason and Luke are already there. I sit down before I realize I forgot my lunch in my locker. I'm not hungry anyway. The invisible fruit salad is still heavy in my stomach.

A few minutes later, Jesse sits next to me and says, "Have y'all had Computer yet today? Did you read that article about the food-poisoning record in Abilene?"

Jason and Luke say they didn't read it. Justin says, "I don't have that class until sixth period."

I stay silent.

Jesse picks up one of his school-issued nachos, and he

shakes it until a glop of chunky, melted cheese drops to his tray. "I doubt they really set the record. This school has poisoned way more people than that." He pops the chip in his mouth, chews it, and swallows. "Anything you want to add, Milo?"

I shake my head. "Nope."

"Nothing?" Jesse says. "Seems like it'd be a terrific opportunity."

This is giving me time?

Jason unwraps a Twinkie and shoves it into his mouth all at once.

"Geez!" says Luke. "That's disgusting."

"Sorry," Jason mumbles, his mouth still full. A crumb flies out and lands in front of me.

I don't waste the opportunity to make Jesse back off. I pick it up and eat it.

"Ewwwww!" Luke says.

Jesse gags, thanks to his easily triggered reactions.

I shrug. "Forgot my lunch."

CHAPTER 18

After school I go straight to detention. I don't care if Jesse waits for me or not.

Today I'm the first one there and the teacher slides over the clipboard on his desk for me to sign in. I point to three computers in the back of the classroom. "Can I use one of those?"

The teacher frowns.

"Please? It's for homework."

He nods. "For homework."

In theory, I'm not lying. It's work for home. Because in last period, I figured out what I've got to do.

I'm doubling down.

If I break the record, then I won't be lying and there will be nothing to confess.

I type in "Bishop Rock and the King of Lighthouses" into the search bar and click on the first web page. I breathe easier when I see the pictures. This is the reminder I needed.

I'll be like the dude who didn't give up when his first lighthouse washed away. I just need to build that second, indestructible lighthouse and everything will be fine.

I minimize that page, go to the internet browser, and type in the address of my family's most-frequented Guinness discussion board. We use this page to find our record attempts. More people come into detention behind me, but I don't turn around.

I go to the Advanced Search button and fill out the electronic form. I click Select All for Type of Event—I don't care if the attempt involves mass participation, animals, or physical activities. I add my zip code and check the box that says I'm willing to travel up to 650 miles. Once I press Enter, it only takes a couple of seconds to give me my narrowed options.

There are fifty-three events fitting my criteria. All I need to do is find the best one.

I rule several of them out immediately. The MOST PEOPLE DRESSED AS MUMMIES and LARGEST FLASH MOB won't happen until next year. I need this by next week. The sooner the better.

After ruling out any of the events that include running a marathon or swimming in freezing water or actual talent, I whittle the list to eleven possibilities.

"That looks promising," somebody says behind me. It's Brandon. He leans over and points to the description of one of the attempts—Lucy the Skateboarding Cocker Spaniel is going to try to break into Guinness by skateboarding through a human tunnel. Otto, the Skateboarding Bulldog of Peru, currently holds the record for skateboarding through thirty sets of legs.

"Thanks for your feedback." I hope he doesn't notice my fingers shaking over the keyboard. "Now go away."

"They sort of make you stay in the room when you're in detention."

I raise my hand. "Excuse me, sir? I'm trying to do my homework, and this kid is bugging me."

"Sit down, please," the teacher says.

"Just helping you out. Chill, Record Breaker."

The nickname makes me want to charge him again. "Why are you even here?"

"Shhhh!" He puts his finger over his lips and loudly whispers, "No talking."

"Do you need another day of detention?" the teacher asks him.

"Nah, I'm good," he says.

When he's gone, I return to my search and go through all the record-breaking possibilities. Guinness has six rules for a record:

1. Must be able to measure it.
2. Must be able to be challenged by other people.
3. Must be able to repeat it.
4. Must be able to prove it.
5. Must have only one thing to measure.
6. Must be the best in the world.

With all this in mind, I hate the conclusion: Brandon is right. The skateboarding dog *is* the best bet.

The official attempt will be in St. Louis this weekend. My parents and I will just have to stand in a row with other people, and the dog will ride through the tunnel of legs.

The hardest part of the entire attempt will be to persuade my parents we need to do it. I print out the picture of Bishop Island and use the paper to write all the details about the skateboarding dog on the back, and stuff it into my back pocket.

CHAPTER 19

By the time I get home, dinner is ready. The beginning of the meal is the clink of forks and scrape of knives on plates. My parents are clearly in the middle of a "discussion."

Mom is the first to speak. "How was school?" she asks me as she cuts her chicken too hard. "We missed seeing Jesse today."

"Yeah, I had to stay after to do some work. He went home."

Dad stabs his peas with his fork.

"Everything okay?" I ask.

Mom wipes her mouth too hard with her napkin. "Yup."

"Perfect," Dad adds.

Mom clears her throat. "What did you stay to work on?"

"Actually," I say, reaching for the paper with the detail of the record attempt in my pocket.

"Are you having trouble in class? Do I need to talk with one of your teachers?" Mom is in full fix-it mode.

"How are your grades looking?" Dad asks.

I must be careful here. Lecturing is Dad's coping mechanism. He's probably hoping I failed a test so he can really let loose. If I haven't though, there's always his standby speeches on "Planning Ahead" and the "Value of Education."

"Nope. None. No tests. I'm doing great in school." Today's detention pops into my head, but I ignore the thought and stuff a bite of chicken in my mouth.

Dad frowns. "You should take smaller bites. You'll end up swallowing air and get indigestion. I read an article about it the other day."

Yup. They are definitely fighting. And there's only one way to end this quickly so I can talk to my parents about more important things.

I put my fork on my plate and scoot back from the table. I can't see the box on the top of the fridge, but I know it lives there. I reach up, and my fingers find the smooth wood. I slide it off and take it back to the table, moving the dishes of food aside to make room.

"Which challenge do you choose?" I ask.

I remove the box's lid.

"I don't think this is necessary," Dad says.

Mom leans forward. "Oh, I think it is."

"You pick, Mom. Sticky notes, clothespins, or spoons?"

"I choose…clothespins. Whoever has the most clothespins on their face in three minutes wins."

"Really? The clothespins?" Dad says. "You didn't lose bad enough last time?"

"Ah, last time you had a beard. That gave you an unfair advantage. I want a rematch."

I take the stopwatch out of the box. "Grab your supplies."

Mom and Dad both slide their plates out of the way, though Dad sighs while he does it. They divide the clothespins between them. Mom reaches over to take three of Dad's. "I'm going to need these. You won't."

I hover my thumb over the Start button on the timer. "As a reminder, the clothespins must be above your jaw-line. None of them can be clipped to your eyelids or ears. They must stay for five seconds or it doesn't count. Ready?" I pause. Mom and Dad both lean forward and hover their hands over the table. "And . . . go!"

My parents snap the pins to their faces. We've all watched the video of Kevin Thackwell winning this challenge with 104 clothespins. Just like Kevin, Mom and Dad start across the jawline. They look like half-wooden lions. From there, they use different strategies. Mom clips hers on the ridge of her eyebrows. Dad makes a second row of a mane.

A pin pops off Dad's face, and Mom says, "See? Not so easy without the beard to hold it, is it?"

I give my parents an extra thirty seconds. "And stop."

They hold up their hands.

"You look ridiculous," Mom says. When she laughs, two clothespins fall. "Those still count!"

Without moving his lips, Dad says, "I look like a winner."

Mom beats Dad by four. Both their faces still have pinch marks.

Dad rubs his hand across his forehead like he's trying to smooth it. "I concede defeat. But I also suspect you've been practicing."

Mom winks at him. "Maybe I have, and maybe I haven't."

"Are y'all officially over your fight now?"

Mom waves my words away. "We weren't fighting. We were having a spirited debate."

"That's right," Dad agrees. "And, honey, what spirit would you say possessed you for the last hour?"

She glares at Dad. "Hush."

Dad closes his eyes and holds out his arms. "Supermean spirit, I demand you leave my wife and let her return to the reasonable lady I married."

Mom swats at his hand.

He pulls his arms back. "Ouch. I see you're still in there."

The plates receive less abuse now. The goofy challenges always work. It's hard to stay mad with clothespins or sticky notes or spoons on your face.

I picture my parents covered in sticky notes so I can be brave. "I need to talk to you both about something."

Mom puts down her fork. Wrinkles appear between her eyebrows. "I knew something was wrong."

"No, it's not like that. I just...I found a record attempt. And I really, really want to do it."

"That's great, Milo!" Dad says. "Way to take initiative."

"The thing is though, we'd have to leave tomorrow."

Dad frowns. "We were supposed to go to Jesse's cross-country race this weekend."

"I know. And it feels like it's rushed. It's just—" My voice shakes. I picture the sticky notes on my face too. "I think it's a sure thing. I *need* to break a record."

"Why, Milo?" Mom puts her hand over mine.

"I just need a win. Please?" I hate the way my voice sounds. I point to the clothespins. "The attempts make everything better. You get that, right?"

"I do," Mom says, and squeezes.

Dad sighs. "Majority wins. What and when and where?"

"St. Louis and this weekend. For Lucy the Skateboarding Cocker Spaniel. I even checked with the airports. We can fly if we don't have time to drive."

"I don't know, Milo," Dad says.

Mom and Dad look at each other from opposite sides of the table. I think they're having a silent conversation like Jesse and I do. If I paid attention, I could probably translate, but I'm too busy crossing my fingers and waiting for an answer.

"Okay." Dad rolls his eyes, but he's smiling. "RSVP on the website and tell them we're in. Let's make this happen."

Relief floods over me. "Thank you. I really do think this could be our win."

"Silly, Milo," Dad says. "A win is just how you define it."

CHAPTER 20

Victory! So far at least.

We are in the car and on our way to meet Lucy the Skateboarding Cocker Spaniel. Tomorrow Lucy will make history as she rides through the legs of thirty-plus people and breaks the current record of longest human tunnel traveled through by a dog skateboarder.

We left our house early this morning. By this time tomorrow, we should be record breakers.

"What do you think it takes to teach a dog to skateboard?" Dad asks as we cross the Texas–Oklahoma state line.

"A dog, for one," I say.

"Do you think any dog would work?" Mom asks.

"Well," Dad says, "it's got to be small enough to go through people's legs but have a big enough brain to learn how to skateboard."

"Good point," Mom says. "How long do you think it takes for a human to learn to ride a skateboard? Probably would take a dog at least twice that."

"Depends on the human," Dad says.

I lean forward. "I say this conversation is pointless unless we have a dog."

Dad glances in the rearview mirror and changes lanes. "Maybe we should get a dog and train it. We could find out that way."

"How about as soon as we win this record, you can ask Lucy's owner," I say. "Then we don't have to guess?"

"Good point. I think I will."

My phone buzzes. It's a text from Jesse. He's bummed we are going to a record attempt instead of his cross-country meet. I reply that it came up super last minute and that I can't talk.

When we get to St. Louis, it's just getting dark. We go straight to the hotel and get pizza delivered for dinner. After we eat, it's time for bed. One more wake up and everything will be fixed.

Mom and Dad doze off quickly. At midnight, I'm still wide awake.

To fall asleep, I count. But instead of fence-jumping sheep, I list off our past record attempts in my head.

After tomorrow, I bet I won't think of all these failures again.

After tomorrow, the past attempts won't even matter.

CHAPTER 21

It's *go* time.

The sun is rising when we pull into the park. There's already a small crowd.

When my parents and I join them, a tall bald dude with glasses shakes my parents' hands. He offers the standard introduction of these Guinness events: name, hometown, and success rate. His name is Jed, he's from Little Rock, and this will be his fourth record.

Mom and Dad give their names and then mine. Mom tells him we're from Dallas, then Dad ends with his standard line. "We don't have a record yet, but that's not for lack of trying!"

"Good morning!" a lady with short blond hair yells into a microphone. She's wearing a navy blue jacket with a small Guinness logo on the right side. She's followed by two guys carrying video equipment. "I'm Robin Green-acre, and I'm lucky enough to be the adjudicator for this spectacular achievement. Are we ready to see Lucy break a record?"

"Absolutely!" Dad yells.

The rest of us clap.

The guy with the huge camera on his shoulder steps back and aims the lens in our direction.

Robin puts her finger to her ear and listens to her earpiece. "I've just got word that Lucy has arrived. She's glad you've all made it and will thank you in licks after her performance."

She pauses to give us a chance to laugh. We do.

"You'll see that there are two long rows of tape on the sidewalk. You'll need to arrange yourself in a single-file line with one of your feet on each length of tape."

We all merge to the sidewalk.

"After you," says an enormous guy in a trucker hat. I wonder if he's ever considered challenging the record as the tallest man.

Dad, Mom, and I end up in the middle of the line. We obey the adjudicator and put one foot on each piece of tape. The result is a long row of people straddling the sidewalk.

"Great!" Robin says. "Now we'll number you off. One thing though. We need to make sure Lucy has plenty of room, so we might ask some of you to step aside."

She makes her way down the line and pulls out two kids and one really short old lady. The guy with the camera follows her. I stand tall as they pass me. The lady tells me I'm number seventeen.

They give person number thirty—a dude with blue hair—a sign to hold so we know when Lucy's tied the record. They line up seven more people behind her in case Lucy can shatter the previous attempt.

"All right, folks," the adjudicator says as she returns to the front of the line. "We're all set. Are you ready to see Lucy?"

We all cheer.

"I can't hear you!" Robin says.

We clap harder. A couple of people scream, "Wahoo!"

Mom nudges me. "Come on. Smile. This is for you."

I force the sides of my mouth up. As soon as we win, I'll really smile.

"Here's the dog of the hour!" Robin says, gesturing to the parking lot.

Lucy bounds toward us. A guy carrying a glittery skateboard follows her.

The dog runs to our human leg tunnel. She jumps and spins and barks.

"Lucy!" calls the skateboard-holding man, "Sit, girl."

The dog obeys, but her nub of a tail shakes so hard, it wiggles her entire body.

"Here," the guy says when he catches up. Lucy listens. She spins twice when she gets to him.

I can barely breathe. This is my chance for redemption.

The guy sets the skateboard down in front of Lucy. Without hesitation, the dog hops on. The board makes it roughly two feet before Lucy jumps off.

The skateboard keeps going and hits the foot of the first person in the line, a guy with spiky hair and approximately thirty-eight million piercings. Piercing dude's hands shoot straight up. "I didn't mean to touch it!"

Was that it?

Was that the attempt?

Surely not. Even *my* family can't lose that quickly.

"It's okay," Robin assures us. "The attempt hasn't officially started."

Lucy's owner gets the board and sets it down again. He puts his foot on it. "Come here, girl!"

She happily obeys.

"Okay," the owner says. "Let's do this."

"We need complete silence," Robin says, "while Lucy makes the official attempt." She kneels down and pets the dog on the head. "Okay, Lucy. Go when ready."

Lucy gets on the skateboard; her owner sets her free. The attempt officially starts.

Lucy comes to the first pair of legs, and...this time she goes through!

She passes under the next set of legs and the next one and the next one.

She'll go through mine next. I hold my breath and stay completely still. She passes through. I turn to watch the rest of her attempt. I clinch my fists, willing her to keep going.

And...she does it! She passes the thirtieth person. The blue-haired dude lifts the sign in victory.

Lucy tied the record! Now she has a chance to break it!

She's still going—through the legs of the extra people lined up. She passes thirty-two, thirty-three!

She rides until she hits the foot of person thirty-six.

Thirty-six! That's five more sets of legs than she needed. World record officially *shattered*!

Lucy's owner runs down the line and meets her as she steps off the board. The dog barks and spins and jumps. She takes all offered treats.

I bet she has no clue what she just did. It doesn't matter though. It's a huge victory—for Lucy the Skateboarding Cocker Spaniel and for ME!

Dad kisses Mom straight on the mouth. He picks me up to hug me even though I'm too big and it's embarrassing.

Everybody is talking at once and saying stuff like, "Did you see that?" and "Thirty-six people. Thirty-six!" and "She did it! So amazing!"

"Thank you all for coming!" Robin Greenacre yells into the microphone.

We all quiet down.

"This is a momentous occasion. And Lucy," she says, turning to the dog. Lucy responds by licking her, and everybody laughs. "Those were some serious skateboarding skills. I didn't know if you were going to make it."

Her owner gives Lucy a rough pat and says, "Ah, I never doubted it."

"And now it's time for the official presentation."

The official presentation! We've never made it this far! *I can't believe this is happening.*

My parents stand next to me with their arms slung around each other. Huge, clownish smiles are plastered on their faces.

This is why we've been chasing these records. For this win. For this feeling I have right now. It's like...it's like...*winning.* As in *not losing.* And it feels *amazing.*

Robin Greenacre holds a framed plaque. I imagine it hanging on our living room wall. No, we'll put it over the fireplace. We'll throw out everything that reminds us of our failed attempts: the Toilet Paper Tower, the rubber-band-ball chairs, the dice, the chopsticks, the dominoes, the soccer balls, the roach costumes, the Smurf costumes, and the M&M's. This attempt is the only one that matters!

"Today Lucy set the new official world record for the longest human tunnel traveled through by a dog skate-boarder. Way to go, Lucy!"

The crowd claps and whoops and whistles. I try to whistle too, but I don't really know how. I just blow a bunch of air.

"This is so great," I tell Dad.

He puts his arm around me and says, "Absolutely excellent."

"And what happens next? Do we get the plaque here, or do they mail it?" I hope they don't have to mail it. I want it now.

"Huh?" Dad says.

"For breaking the record. The plaque. How do we get it?"

Robin Greenacre hands the plaque to Lucy's owner. "Congratulations, Lucy the Skateboarding Cocker Spaniel. You are now part of Guinness. Welcome to the family. And, to the rest of you, thank you all for coming to support Lucy!"

"Wait. They'll mail it to us, then? Our certificate?" I ask Dad. "For the record we broke."

"Bud," Dad says, putting his hand on my shoulder. "We didn't break a record. Lucy did. We were participants."

"Yes," I agree. "We *par-tic-i-pa-ted* in breaking a record. We won. *Finally.*"

Dad's face softens. I don't like it.

"We participated when *Lucy* broke the record," he says. "It's hers. Not ours."

I shake my head. "No."

Dad tilts his head to the side. I recognize his expression: It's pity.

"What's wrong?" Mom says.

"We didn't break a record," I tell her, waiting for her to react.

"I know. But we got to see Lucy break one."

"Seriously, Mom? Seriously?"

"Yes, *seriously*, Milo. What is wrong now? We did exactly what you wanted us to do. We drove all the way to St. Louis. For you."

"But we were supposed to get a record. We were supposed to *win*."

I don't understand. Or I do, but I don't *want* to.

I can't be here for another second; I walk away and head straight to the car. It takes me a minute to realize my parents aren't following me.

I sit on the curb next to the parking lot and pull grass out of the cracks. I tear the blades to shreds.

When my parents finally show up, they are laughing, talking, totally unconcerned that I've been missing.

"Do you want to see the picture?" Mom asks Dad.

He takes her phone. "This is greatness."

When he hands it back to her, she asks me, "Do you want to see? Dad took a picture with Lucy. She gave him a wet willy with her tongue right as I got the shot."

I don't respond.

Mom shrugs and puts her phone back in her purse. She and Dad get into the car. I'm still on the sidewalk when the engine starts.

I bet they'd leave me here if they could.

I get into the back seat and slam the door.

"That was stupid," I say.

Mom turns to look at me. "Is there something you want to talk about, Milo?"

"We should give up."

"Huh?" Dad sounds confused—like he thinks I'm speaking gibberish.

"We are never going to break a world record."

"Sure we will, bud," Dad says.

"But even if we didn't, wouldn't that be okay?" Mom says.

I almost laugh. Almost. *"No."*

"I think you're upset and probably tired," Mom says.

"Why don't you lean back and rest a little, then we can talk after."

I listen, but I don't rest. For the first time, I know exactly what I need: to stop the record attempts.

I take out my phone and pull up Jesse's texts. I have five unread messages from him.

Jesse: How's it going?

Jesse: Headed home from the meet.

Jesse: I won again.

Jesse: Did you break a record?

Jesse: When are you coming back?

I reply: We didn't break a record.

I'm about to put my phone down, but I decide to send one last text. I need to tell somebody: And I am officially done trying.

CHAPTER 22

When I wake up the next morning, I know how it must feel to be the heaviest man alive, because getting out of bed seems nearly impossible.

"Milo!" Mom says when I walk into the kitchen. "We've been waiting for you." She slides a chair out from the table. "Sit." Then she calls to my dad, "Honey, he's here."

Dad bounds into the kitchen with a stopwatch in his hand. "Let's do this."

Mom plunks down three glass ketchup bottles. She gives Dad and me a straw—I take it even though I don't know what is happening yet—and she keeps one for herself.

"I think we should do this one at a time," she says as she picks up the camera. "Who's first?"

"I'll go," Dad says.

I'm obviously missing something. Like having normal parents.

"Wait. What's happening?" I ask.

"Simple." Dad holds up his ketchup bottle. "All we have to do is drink this bottle of ketchup with a straw in under twenty-five seconds."

We're barely home from our last disaster, and they are already on to the next one. "Not happening."

"It's okay, Milo," Mom says. "It's totally safe."

Dad laughs and shakes his head. "Remember how when we tried to break the fastest-water-drinking record, it gushed out of your nose, Milo? That was *hilarious*."

Water pouring out of your nose burns, actually. Not funny at all. But I don't let myself get distracted. "I told you we should stop. I'm not doing this anymore."

Dad tilts his head like he's genuinely confused. "But if Richard Browning gave up, he wouldn't have a flight suit."

"The thing is, we are never going to break a record." I clench my hand into a fist. "We should stop trying if we're never going to win."

Mom nods. "Okay," she says, "I get that. But what if breaking a record isn't the point?"

"Hey, we're more likely to get a win than somebody sitting on their couch." Dad pauses. "Unless that could break a record. Hey! Do you think that could break a record? I'd be up for trying it!" He tears the wrapper off the straw.

"Honey," Mom says to Dad, "maybe we should pause and talk to Milo right now."

"Does that mean we aren't doing the ketchup drinking? Because I've been looking forward to it."

I shrug like I don't care. Because I don't. "You can do whatever you want. But I'm out."

Mom nods. "Okay. If that's what you want to do. You can take a break."

"But..." Dad frowns. "I don't have to take a break, right?"

Mom rolls her eyes and smiles at me. I force myself to smile back.

"Start rolling," Dad says.

Mom lifts up the camera. "And...go."

"Hello out there to all my fans," Dad says, even though nobody will see this video. "Today I'm attempting to beat the record for drinking a bottle of ketchup in under twenty-five seconds. As you can see, I have an ordinary bottle of ketchup that I'm opening. Listen for the suction-breaking pop." He unscrews the lid. "See? Brand-new. Never been opened. And I have a handy-dandy straw."

I leave the kitchen before he starts. I keep my eyes down as I walk to my room. This is the only way our house looks normal. No toilet-paper towers. No rubber-band-ball chairs at the kitchen table. No oversized glass jars along the back of the kitchen counter holding a growing collection of candy wrappers.

Leaving the record breaking behind is now *my* newest attempt. And this time I won't fail.

CHAPTER 23

I wait for Jesse on the sidewalk in front of his house on Monday morning.

"Hey," I say, walking up to meet him at the door.

He jumps and drops his key on the porch.

"Sorry. Didn't mean to scare you."

He picks up the key and shoves it in his pocket. "What are you doing here?"

We usually meet in front of my house, since he has to pass by it on the way to school.

"Left early today. Thought I'd come meet you."

We start walking. Jesse is going faster than normal.

"How'd the meet go this weekend? Congrats on the win."

"Thanks," he says, almost like he's sad about it.

"Awesome," I say. And I mean it. Maybe since I won't always be failing now, I won't be jealous of Jesse. This is good. "So. I'll come clean today." Maybe I won't be the record breaker, but at least I won't be the liar.

I feel lighter when I say this. Free or something. Taller, even, without the weight of failure dragging me down.

When we push through the doors of the school, the heater blows in my face. We split up so Jesse can go to his locker and I can go to mine. When I open the metal door, a small piece of paper falls to my feet and I pick it up. It's folded into a little square and has my name on the outside. I'm about to open it, but Jesse is already next to me again. I shove the paper into my pocket, stuff my backpack inside the locker, and we head to first period.

My new attitude must be showing. People can tell I'm different because on the way to class, my line of sight lands on two girls I know, Desiree and Arwyn, and they make it obvious they are looking at me, like they want me to see them. Maybe one of them put the note in my locker.

"Hey." I lean toward Jesse and whisper, "I think those girls are looking at us."

"Maybe," Jesse says like he's nervous about the attention. I'm the one who should be nervous. He should be used to the attention by now.

When we get to first period, I'm getting out my pencil and math book when Jesse comes over to my desk. "Milo, I've gotta talk to you."

He looks sick or something. I stand up in case he needs to sit in my chair. "You okay?"

"Yeah, but—"

"What's up, Record Breaker?" Brandon says, walking through the middle of Jesse and me.

"Jerk," I say under my breath. Maybe without other distractions I can put my free time toward battling Brandon. I haven't even retaliated since the kangaroo incident. I'm slipping.

The bell rings, and Mrs. Docet tells everybody to go to their desks.

"I'll tell you later," Jesse says.

"You sure?"

"Yeah." He trudges back to his desk.

In the middle of first period, I start falling asleep, and

I shift in my chair to wake up. My pocket crinkles, and I remember the note.

Underneath my desk, I unfold the paper, slowly so it doesn't make noise.

The note is not from Desiree or Arwyn.

There's one line written in dull pencil: *Hey Record Breaker. Everybody knows you lied.*

I recognize the nickname. Record Breaker. The note came from Brandon.

I crumple it in my hand. Even when it's a tiny ball, I keep squeezing it.

The teacher starts talking, but I can't pay attention.

No. Today is not supposed to go this way.

I am moving on. Brandon can't take me down.

Plus, it's my turn to get him back. That's how we do this. I get him, then he gets me, then I get him again, and so on.

I can't think. I can't listen.

Detention. He saw me researching the attempts. He figured it out.

Brandon told everybody. Because why wouldn't he? He's probably been waiting for this moment for years. He is going for the ultimate win against me. And even if I'm ready to give up the records, he's not going to let this go.

After class I'm the first one out the door.

I don't wait for Jesse, and I *definitely* don't wait for Brandon to get a chance to enjoy his victory.

CHAPTER 24

E vel Knievel broke the record for most bone fractures with 433 breaks. During Knievel's last stunt, he jumped into a shark-filled tank and earned a concussion and two broken arms for his attempt. That had to hurt *way* more than being outdone by your bully. This is what I keep telling myself anyway.

During second period, I put my head on the desk so nobody will talk to me. Mrs. Pham asks if I'm sick. Later, in the hallway between second and third period, Jason comes up to me and says, "I heard you lied about the record thing."

"Yeah. I did."

I wait. So does he.

"Any other questions?" I ask.

"Oh." Jason takes a step back. "I guess not."

When I get to fourth period, I sit at my normal computer and wiggle the mouse. My screen pops on.

Right before the bell rings for lunch, Jesse says, "So, you know, are we okay, then?"

"Yeah," I say.

"You're not mad at me at all?"

"Jesse this isn't about *you*."

"It's just, I'm sorry," he continues. "I shouldn't have said anything. I was mad, I guess. And then Nina and Pops were supposed to come to my meet, but then they went to St. Louis with you. I didn't know you were so upset until I got your text. And I didn't know you were planning on telling everybody the truth today."

"Wait," I say. My brain struggles—or maybe it is refusing—to comprehend what Jesse's saying. "You told everybody I lied about the records?"

"All I did was tell the truth."

"You told the truth. To everybody. Right. Okay. Did you write the note too?"

Jesse frowns. "What note?"

I blink hard and rub my forehead.

"Milo. I'm so sorry. You are mad, aren't you?"

The bell rings, but neither of us stand up.

" 'Mad' is not the right word. I'm..."

I can't think of the word I want to use. I'm angry. I'm embarrassed. I'm betrayed. I'm somebody who has lost everything he thought he could count on.

"Bye, Jesse."

I get up and leave.

CHAPTER 25

I don't sit at my usual spot in the cafeteria.

I'm not hungry anyway. I'm about to skip lunch and head for the library when I see Brandon sitting alone. I walk over to his table and sit across from him. "Two things," I say.

He squints at me. "Why are you here?"

"The first. I'm not fighting with you anymore. You've officially won."

"Can't wait to see what happens when I let my guard down. I see you're moving on to the long con."

I ignore him. I wouldn't believe him if he surrendered either.

"And the second is a question. Why did you write the note?"

"What note?"

I roll my eyes. "I'm not a dummy. Neither are you."

Brandon leans forward with huge eyes. "We're done with the pranking and now a compliment. Are you trying to be my friend, Record Breaker? Okay, then. I accept."

I close my eyes and let myself fall forward until my forehead is on the table.

"Whoa. I didn't mean to break you." He leans forward and whispers. "You okay, man?"

No. I'm not. If Brandon Rosten is worried about me, then obviously I am not fine at all.

"Sit up and glare at me. Then I'll know you aren't dying."

I do what he asks.

"Thanks," he says. "I feel better."

Actually, I do too.

Brandon crunches a carrot and makes me wait while he chews and swallows. "Yeah. I wrote the note." I glance at my normal table. Jesse's already there—and so are all the people he blabbed to.

"Why?"

"Hey. Who are you?" a guy in a gray hoodie says. He sits down in the chair next to me.

"This is Milo," Brandon says. "He didn't break a record."

The guy shrugs and says, "Okay. Neither did I. I'm Jaden."

Desiree and a guy from my fifth-period science class, Greg, take two of the other chairs. When Benjamin—a kid who went to the same elementary school as Brandon and me—sits across from us at the table he says, "Whoa, what is happening here? Are y'all, like, friends now or something?"

Brandon throws a wadded napkin at him. "Don't be weird, Ben."

Benjamin throws the napkin back at Brandon.

"Anybody want this?" Brandon says, holding up a sandwich.

When nobody claims it, he tosses it in front of me. "You don't have any lunch. Eat this." Desiree slides over a cheese stick and Greg gives me chips.

I glance over at Jesse. He's cracking up—probably about something Jason said.

I open the baggie and take a bite of the sandwich. I don't even care that Brandon probably contaminated it.

"So the Ping-Pong table gets to my house next week," Brandon says. "Who wants to be the first to lose to me."

"Can't," Greg says. "I've got football."

"I can," Desiree says, "but I don't want to."

Brandon rolls his eyes. "What about you, Record Breaker?"

A father-son team holds the record for LONGEST TABLE TENNIS RALLY. Table tennis is just another name for Ping-Pong. Daniel and Peter Ives hit the ball back and forth for eight hours, forty minutes, and five seconds. When I was six years old, Dad bought a Ping-Pong table. He said we'd practice and break the Ives' record. We didn't. The longest we ever went was two hours, sixteen minutes, and eight seconds.

"Maybe," I say.

"Okay," he says.

"If that really happens, I'll come too, in case y'all need a referee," Benjamin says.

I want to tell him not to make any plans. Brandon only asked because I'm right here. It's not like we're friends now or anything.

Except maybe we could be. Maybe everything is different now.

CHAPTER 26

"**D**on't give up now! You are so close," Mom says when I come downstairs after I've finished my homework. At first I think she's talking to me, but then she adds, "Just eight more rolls!"

"Okay," Dad says, his voice strained. "Do it. Add one."

In the living room, Dad is standing with his arms out like he's trying to balance. He's got six rolls of toilet paper stacked on his head. Mom is at the highest rung of the ladder and carefully adding another roll to the top.

"You getting it?" Dad asks. He looks up without tilting his head.

"Almost got it. But...hold on." Mom climbs down

off the ladder, moves it over about three inches, and climbs up again. "Okay. Now I can reach you."

"Hey, bud!" Dad says when he sees me. "Check me out."

"Oh, good. You're here, Milo. You can hand me the rolls," Mom says.

I pretend I didn't hear her. "I'll go set the table."

I leave before Mom can argue.

Dad ends up balancing a total of eight rolls of toilet paper. A whopping six short of the goal.

"I know we thought it would be better inside," Dad says at dinner. "But maybe I need more room to move so I can balance."

"But the wind will be a factor outside. Oh, you know what?" Mom hits her palm to her head. "I think I forgot to turn off the air conditioner. I bet those drafts make a vortex near the vaulted ceilings. What do you think, Milo?"

"Who knows," I say.

Mom sighs.

Dad clears his throat. "Milo, we've got a surprise for you."

I put down my fork when I notice the fake smile

spread across Mom's face. I know I won't like what they say next.

Mom leans forward. "We know you were upset when the record with Lucy didn't work out. So we've got a plan. It's a sure thing. We're going to Kansas for our next record-breaking attempt."

"Kansas!" Dad says. "That's *amazing*!"

"No," I say. "I'm not going."

Mom tries to smile even bigger, but it's more of a wide-eyed grimace. "And guess what? We're flying!"

"We're using an airplane though," Dad says. "I looked into a family set of flight suits, and they are still too expensive."

Mom laughs. "Plane tickets are already bought. We're going next Friday morning, and we'll break the record for most people howling like a wolf at one time. What do you think, Milo?"

For a second, I'm tempted.

The rush of a new attempt makes me forget—just for a bit—my new reality. But then Dad adds, "This will be our big win!"

And that settles it. "No. Because we've all thought that. At least a hundred times before. And we've failed.

Every single time." I shake my head. "I'm sorry, but I'm not going."

Dad frowns. "That's not really a choice you can make. Right?" He looks at Mom. "Is it?"

"I know you're upset," Mom says, standing up. "Clothespins, sticky notes, or spoons?" She gets the box from the top of the fridge.

"None of it." I push away from the table, and the chair feet scrape against the floor. "Can I go to my room? I'm not hungry."

"But—" Dad starts.

"Yes," Mom interrupts. "As long as you rinse your plate and put it in the dishwasher."

I stand up and scrape my uneaten food in the trash. I leave my parents—Dad at the table and Mom standing there holding the challenge box. I feel them watching me like I'm going to change my mind and turn around and tell them I was just kidding.

Lying on my bed and staring at the ceiling, I can't stay still. I'm itchy. Antsy. I feel like a caterpillar that got stuck in its cocoon.

I move to my desk. Looking for something to do, I open the drawers. The pencils and papers slide around.

In the third drawer, I find the folded paper with Bishop Rock on one side and the jotted info from Lucy the Skateboarding Cocker Spaniel's attempt on the other.

I smooth the paper onto my desk.

I hate this dumb island with its dumb lighthouse.

I pick up the paper and tear it in half.

It makes me feel better.

So I rip and rip and rip until the paper is in shreds on my desk and I can breathe again.

CHAPTER 27

The guy who broke the record for LONGEST TIME BREATH HELD VOLUNTARILY secured his victory in twenty-four minutes.

The guy that broke the record for LONGEST MARATHON ON A ROLLER COASTER rode that thing for over four hundred hours.

I've set two of my own records recently: the longest time without talking to Jesse and the longest time without an attempt to break a world record. Both have been seven days. I consider breaking that not-talking-to-Jesse streak just so he and I can both be shocked that I am willingly going to Brandon's house today.

After school, I meet Brandon by the flagpole to wait for his brother to pick us up. "Benjamin had to bail," he says.

I nod and fiddle with my jacket zipper.

Brandon checks his watch and his phone a bunch. Finally, he says, "There he is." A green Jeep pulls up in front of us. "Come on."

I follow him. He climbs in the front, and I get in the back.

The driver, Brandon's brother, nods at me. "Hey."

"Hi," I reply, amazed I can sound so dumb with a single word.

The car starts pulling forward when Brandon says, "This is Hunter."

"Cool," I say. Hunter almost makes Brandon look scrawny.

"Who are you?" Hunter asks. He glances in the rear-view mirror and pulls out of the school's drive.

"I'm Milo."

Hunter stops in the middle of the street. A car behind us blares its horn for a solid three seconds before swerving around.

Brandon hits his brother on the shoulder. "What are you doing, Hunter? Go!"

Hunter starts driving again and adjusts the rearview mirror to look at me. "Why is this guy in my car?"

"Because he is," Brandon answers.

"I can walk home," I say. "Just pull over and I'll get out."

"No," Brandon says. "It's fine. We're cool now."

Hunter laughs. "You're *cool* now? Didn't you *just* get detention because of him? Geez, Brandon." He shakes his head. "You're such a wimp."

"What's he talking about?" I ask Brandon.

He rolls his eyes. "Don't worry about it."

"Oh. Are you taking him home so you can beat him up with no witnesses?" Hunter hits Brandon on the back. "Good thinking."

Every muscle in my body tenses. "What?"

Brandon shakes his head. "Don't listen to him." He hits his brother again. "Shut up, Hunter."

We turn down an alley, and Hunter pulls into the driveway of a huge white-brick house. There are four separate garage doors. The last garage door opens, and he drives through.

Once the door closes behind us, Hunter turns in his seat. He looks at me and then at Brandon. "So, you want help?"

"Go away," Brandon says.

"Whatever," Hunter says as he gets out of the car and slams the door.

"Come on," Brandon says.

I hesitate. "You sure?"

"Since when have you been afraid of me? Let's go." I leave the safety of the Jeep and follow Brandon inside. After a hallway where we leave our shoes, we walk through the living room. It's massive. The floors are dark wood; the couch and chairs are all smooth, tan leather. There is not a single item on any of the side tables. The room has the same don't-touch feeling as a museum. Everything is so perfect. So clean. And so *not* like my house.

Brandon goes straight up the stairs. I don't touch the rails—they are made from a solid piece of perfect glass. I don't want to leave fingerprints. Or maybe I should leave evidence that I was here.

The second story of Brandon's house feels more lived in. There's a big open area. Here the carpet is worn, the built-in shelves are stuffed with games, and the TV— along with, like, every video game system in existence— is hung above a tangle of cords.

The Ping-Pong table stands in the center of the room. Brandon grabs a paddle from the top and hands it to me.

"When you chill out enough to move your arms again," Brandon says, "I'll serve."

I set my paddle on the table and shrug off my backpack.

"Your house is...nice."

"It's my parents' house. I just live here."

"Got it," I say. "Also, your brother hates me."

Brandon nods. "He does. But it's sweet how I know he cares about me." He lines up in front of the table and serves the ball.

I grab my paddle just in time to hit it back.

"Are you going to, you know, explain any more?"

"Nah." He shakes his head. "Don't think I will."

We volley two more times before he misses.

He bounces the ball to me. I serve, and he misses again. Then he serves. I hit it back and get another point.

"You're pretty good at this," he says.

"You're not."

We rally a few more times, and right when the winning point is supposed to be mine, Brandon catches the ball in his hand. "Look, don't worry about Hunter."

"What does he even mean that you just got detention because of me?"

"He picks me up after school, so I had to tell him why I'd be late. I told him it was because you *tattled* on me." Brandon makes air quotes with his fingers when he says "tattled."

"Why?"

"Because I couldn't tell him I told on myself. He wouldn't understand."

This is still not making any sense. "What are you talking about?"

He shrugs. "I was in detention because I confessed that I messed with your presentation."

I shake my head. "Wait. Why would you do that?"

"Because I was just messing around. Getting you back after the thing in math."

"No, I mean, why would you turn yourself in?"

"Because I didn't know you'd go caveman and get in trouble." He shrugs. "I sort of thought you'd roll with it. You always find a way to win against me, after all. Sort of what makes you an effective bully."

"Um. What? I have *never* bullied you."

"Um. Yes, you have. Since, like, the second grade."

"That is so not true. I was never the bully. We had a mutual dislike."

Brandon shrugs. "Eventually. But at first, it was all you. And, like I said, you always win."

That's not how it happened. He's changing the story.

Or maybe he's not. I've been wrong about everything else lately. Could I be wrong about this too?

"I thought I was doing the right thing. Jesse needed me to have his back."

"I know."

"Can I ask a question though? Why did you take the ring? I mean the kid's dad had just died."

Brandon pushes his hand through his hair. "So that I could forever be defined by something I did in second grade."

"I'm serious."

"I know. But I wasn't thinking like that. I was jealous, I guess. My dad was gone, and my mom was too. They worked all the time. But Jesse got all the attention, and that day, he got to have the ring too. So when mine broke, I took his. Stupid little-kid logic. I wish I never did it." Brandon picks his paddle up. "Can we play now or what?"

"Yeah," I say. I'm about to serve when I stop. "Hey, Brandon?"

"Yeah?"

"I'm sorry."

"You know what I like about you, Record Breaker? Right or wrong, you go all in. Now, let's play until I beat you."

CHAPTER 28

Brandon's right—I do go all in.

Which is why I've decided that it isn't enough for *me* to stop the attempts. My parents need to stop them too. I'm saving them from themselves.

Last night I went to my parents' office and found a copy of the flight reservations on their desk. I typed in the web address of the airline in the search bar, and on the website, I clicked the Cancel Flights button. After thirteen failed attempts at logging in, the site blocked me from trying again.

That may have been a dead end, but I have a plan B.

This morning, right after the announcements, I tell

my teacher I need to go see the principal. I know Mr. Amondo will be there, since we just heard him on the intercom.

His office is open, and he's at his desk. I knock on the doorframe. "Yes. Come in," he says.

I sit in the same chair as last time. "I need to talk to you."

He leans back. "Okay."

For a tiny instant, I feel a flash of guilt, like I'm betraying my parents. But really, I'm doing this for them too. "My mom took me out of school again. A couple of weeks ago."

He nods.

"And you asked about stuff. At home? You were right. Something is going on. And I'm worried I might get behind in school. So I was wondering if maybe you could talk to my parents? Tell my mom and dad I can't miss any more days?"

His eyebrows push together.

I continue. "Because I don't think my absences should be excused actually. I'm missing school because they want to break records."

"Break records?"

"Yes. World records. Like flash-mob dancing and toilet-paper stacking and stuff."

He rubs his chin. "I don't believe that would be excused."

"Yeah." I'm in the odd position of being both the tattler and the tattlee. "Is there a way to let, uh, my parents know? I told them, but . . ."

"Yes." He writes something on a yellow sticky note. "Is there anything else?"

"And is it okay if maybe you don't tell them that I told you?"

He's still writing and doesn't look up at me. "I'll see what I can do."

"Okay." I get up to leave. Pausing at the door, I add, "Thanks."

He nods and straightens his Principal of the Year plaque. "Hurry up and get back to class."

CHAPTER 29

You're acting weird," Brandon tells me after school. We're playing foosball.

"Weird how?"

"I don't know." He spins his guys really fast. "Not talking. Sort of twitchy."

"Oh. Sorry." I shake my head to try to reset my thoughts. The guilt from talking to the principal is getting to me. My shoulders are so tight, it feels like they're next to my ears.

"Does this have something to do with the records?"

I step back, and Brandon scores. "Why? What did you hear?"

"Nothing. Just trying to figure out what is bugging you. Like I said, today you're weird."

I spin my row of guys and hit the ball toward his goal. Brandon stops me from scoring with his last set of defenders.

"I don't even do the records anymore."

"Okay. So, what do you do now?"

"Besides beat you at foosball and Ping-Pong?"

Brandon snorts. "Besides that."

"I don't know." I spin my guys again and score. He takes the ball and puts it back on the table.

I block another one of his shots.

"Have you thought about trying cross-country? We're short a few runners. Plus, you have the same genetics as Jesse, so you'd probably smoke most of us. Not me. But, you know, others."

I tense when he says my ex–best friend's name and miss a chance to block my goal. Brandon scores again.

"You're just trying to distract me so you can win, aren't you?"

"I am if it works." Brandon shrugs. "Hunter says you're only hanging out with me so you can use my stuff."

"That's not true."

"That's what I told him." Brandon crosses his arms. "But then I started thinking about it. And I think maybe you're just using me because you're bored without the records or because you and Jesse aren't friends anymore."

I score on him this time. He steps back from the table, but he doesn't get the ball out of his goal. "You want to know why I wrote that note?"

It takes me a second to push past all the thoughts in my head to remember what he's talking about. "Okay."

"Jesse told me you lied about the records at the cross-country meet."

I abandon the foosball table and sit on the couch. "I know. He told everybody."

"Yeah. I know. But at first he only told me."

That doesn't make sense. They aren't even friends. "Why?"

"I think he thought I'd tell everybody else. Then he wouldn't have to, you know? I didn't say anything though. Then when we were coming home on the bus, he told everybody. He made, like, a big announcement."

I can imagine it exactly—Jesse with his first-place medal around his neck, standing in the aisle and telling everybody the truth about me.

"Your family *should* have your back. The way he did it wasn't cool—at least you and I have always been up front. That's how you should take somebody down. Not behind their back. So I wrote the note."

"Well. Thanks, I guess."

"Jesse asked me about you in cross-country today," Brandon says as he turns on the TV with the remote.

"What'd he say?"

He shrugs. "Just asked how you were. He may have been messing with me. Or maybe he really wanted to know. It just got me thinking, maybe you guys are setting me up, you know?" He clicks through the channels. "You know that story about the ants and the grasshopper? Where the ants spend the whole winter getting their food, but the grasshopper goofs around? Then when winter comes the grasshopper needs food, but the ants won't give him any, so he starves."

"This conversation has taken a turn."

"My dad says the grasshopper should have been able to trick the ant family out of all their food. He says the grasshopper deserves to starve."

I turn to look at him. "Brandon, that's kind of . . . sad."

He shrugs. "It is what it is. But are you and Jesse messing with me?"

"Wait." I shake my head. "No."

"Okay, then." He changes the channels and stares at the TV. "Just wanted to make sure I wasn't being tricked."

"I can say with complete and total honesty, you are a clever grasshopper."

"Thanks, man. I'm glad you noticed."

CHAPTER 30

The world's LARGEST MACARONI AND CHEESE record was set in New Orleans in 2010. It was 2,469 pounds of gooey goodness. My family uses the same recipe—scaled down—on Tuesdays.

Usually the mac 'n' cheese is perfect. Today, it's on fire. Literally.

As soon as I walk through the door of my house, the hazy living room attacks me. The smell burns my throat and makes me cough.

"Mom? Dad?" I yell, but they don't answer.

I throw down my backpack and run into the kitchen right as the alarm starts screaming.

Smoke streams out of the top of the oven. The flames light up on the other side of the glass door.

"*Mom!*" I yell louder this time. "*Dad!*"

"Get back, Milo!" Mom yells, running into the kitchen. Dad is right behind her. The alarm still blares.

"It's on fire!" Mom says when she sees the oven.

"Don't open it!" Dad says. He steps up onto a chair and then onto the kitchen table.

"Dad! What are you *doing*?"

He plows into the middle of Toilet Paper Tower. The entire top half tumbles to the floor.

Dad burrows through the middle of the bottom half. He has obviously lost his mind.

"Call 911," I say over the noise.

Mom has her phone in her hand. She looks around in a panic. "But I don't want anybody else to see the kitchen like this. It's a mess."

"Almost . . . got it," Dad says. His voice is muffled. We can't see him anymore. He's in the center of the Tower.

Then he busts out the other side with a fire extinguisher in his hands. The rolls scatter. Some skid over the top of the table and land at my feet.

He puts the extinguisher between his knees and pulls

the pin out of the top. "Okay. When I count to three, open the door of the oven and stand back!"

"That'll ruin dinner," Mom yells over the alarm. "All that good cheese."

"Mom! It's on fire!" I grab the handle of the oven.

"One. Two. Three!"

I yank open the door and rush out of the way. Dad sprays the extinguisher and a white cloud fills the entire oven—though honestly, when I opened the door there was only a tiny flame on top of the charred mac 'n' cheese.

But the fire is definitely out now.

The air is foggy. Fine white powder lands on the countertops and the floor. Finally, the alarm stops.

Dad steps back to survey the oven. He lifts the nozzle and gives one more squirt before he puts the fire extinguisher next to his feet, wipes his hand across his forehead, and says, "I guess it's pizza night."

"We should charge it to Mr. Amondo," Mom says. "And make him clean up this mess."

"Wait. What? Why my principal?"

"Because this is his fault." She holds up the phone. "We were talking to him, and he distracted us. He called. Just to tell us something *ridiculous*."

Dad starts stacking the toilet paper rolls. "He says

your absences for record breaking will no longer be excused."

"As if he can make that call!" Mom shakes her head. She sets the phone on the counter and starts scooping up the white powder in her hands.

"He said if you miss more school, we'll have to go to truancy court or you'll have to repeat the grade." Dad doesn't seem mad—more resigned maybe.

"Ridiculous!" Mom flings the powder into the kitchen sink.

"We'll figure something out," Dad says.

I try to stop the shaking in my voice when I ask, "How did he even know about the records?"

Dad lifts his hands. "He just kept repeating, 'It has come to my attention.'"

"Well," Mom says. "It's come to *my* attention that all three of us will march in there tomorrow and we will tell him this is *not* okay."

"Please, no."

Mom shakes her head. "This is just unacceptable. They can't tell us that you can't miss school. You're *our* child."

If I walk in with them tomorrow, Mr. Amondo will definitely let them know I tipped him off. I'm not ready for that. Plus, it won't do any good. They'll still make me do the records. I need them to think it is their idea they quit.

"You can go to Kansas. Do the record thing. I'll stay here. He's probably just worried because I'm behind in school anyway. Almost failing, actually."

Dad frowns. "Milo, you know you can't stay home alone. And since when are you failing?"

"*Almost* failing. I just have to do some makeup work. I'll stay at Allie's," I say before considering that staying with my sister also means staying with Jesse.

"Your principal should not be able to tell us what our family can and cannot do," Mom says. She steps forward like she's ready to go talk to him right now.

"But if I end up failing, you'll prove him right. Here." I take my phone out of my pocket and dial Allie's number. When she answers, I say, "Can I stay with you Friday and Saturday night?"

I give my parents a thumbs-up when she says yes.

Dad holds out his hand. "Let me talk to her."

Five minutes later, it is official. My sister has saved me. Surely I can ignore Jesse for two days. We've barely noticed each other for the past two weeks.

CHAPTER 31

My parents left for Kansas this morning. I stop by my house after school and take as long as possible packing my clothes to stay at Allie's. When that doesn't waste as much time as I planned, I straighten up my bathroom. Then, I go through my closet like Mom's always asking me to do.

Normally, this stuff takes about a million years, but today it fills only mere seconds. Next, I watch a YouTube video of dogs who can't catch food in their mouths. As soon as I finish, a video about dogs who walk on two legs pops up; I play that one too. Seven videos later, I come out of my binge-watching haze. It's almost dark outside.

I've missed a text and three calls from Allie. I reply to my sister that I'm on my way; I grab my bag and go.

"Hey, you," Allie calls out when I walk into her house. She's sitting on the couch and reading a book. She looks at her watch. "A little late, aren't we?"

"Sorry. Had to take care of some stuff."

"Uh-huh," she says in a momish-way that means she doesn't believe me. "Jesse's out until later. I have food for you." She smiles and raises her eyebrows. "And something else too. Follow me."

We go into the kitchen, and Allie takes a covered plate out of the fridge. She removes the foil and hands it to me. "You like spaghetti, right? Put it in the microwave. Use a paper towel so it doesn't splatter though. Heat it for two minutes."

"Yes, ma'am," I say. Mainly because Allie hates it.

She gives me the side eye. "If you act like I'm your mom, I'll treat you like I am. Which would be unfortunate because then I couldn't encourage you to eat these." She plops a clear plastic bag full of small red peppers on the kitchen island.

"What's that?"

"What is the hottest pepper in the world?"

"The Carolina Reaper."

Allie crosses her arms and smirks.

"There is no way you would get a Carolina Reaper."

"Or would I?" She raises her eyebrows twice.

I shake my head and put the spaghetti in the microwave without the paper towel to see what she'll do. She must be committed to being the sister-type Allie right now because she only crinkles her nose and doesn't say a thing about the inevitable mess.

"If you try it, I'll eat one too," she says.

Guinness says the California Reaper is the HOTTEST CHILI PEPPER. I've thought of chomping one before – just to say I could. Then I watched the YouTube videos. Anybody who tries it turns sweaty and red. Grown men cry, people faint, ambulances are called.

Allie is obviously as out of touch with reality as our parents.

"Trust me," she says. "I've got milk. And ice cream. It's supposed to help the heat. I'll go first."

My sister takes a pepper out of the bag and brings it to the sink to wash it.

She comes back to the island. "Do you want to video this? Count me down from three."

"You really shouldn't eat that," I tell her.

"It'll be fun."

"You really don't get how hot that is."

She shoos my words away. "Stop being such a worrywart."

"The fact that you just said worrywart..."

Allie tips her head back and holds the pepper above her mouth. "Ready."

"Stop." She has no idea what she's doing. "I've moved on. I'm not even trying to break the stupid records anymore."

Allie pulls the pepper away from her mouth and looks at me. "What?"

"I've moved on."

She drops the pepper onto the counter. I relax. For a second.

"I really hate the phrase 'move on,'" she says in disgust. "Do you know how many times I've heard I should move on?" Her face softens, and her eyes get all watery. "What if I don't want to forget about Todd?"

I cringe. "Allie. I promise I wasn't talking about Todd. I was only talking about the records. Please don't cry."

She wipes her face. "I'm not. I just got some pepper juice in my eye." Allie shakes her head. "It's fine. I'm fine. You just said something I didn't want to think about. *Moving on*," she says, putting her fingers in air quotes. She clears her throat and smooths her hair back with her hands. "Sorry. Didn't mean to lose it in front of you."

I don't know what to say to that. But I don't have to come up with anything, because she continues, "So, I respect your decision. No more record attempts. Right after this one."

Before I can stop her, she grabs the pepper, puts it in her mouth, and yanks out the stem.

"Allie! No! What are you doing?"

"It's fine," she says with her mouth full. Then she chews more, and her eyes get big. "Oh my gosh!" She fans her fingers in front of her mouth. "*Oh my gosh!* Hot! So hot!"

I run to her refrigerator and get the milk. "Drink this."

She doesn't even get a glass. Just chugs it straight out of the gallon. The milk streams out the sides of her mouth.

"Come on, Milo!" she says when she pulls the gallon away long enough to catch her breath. "You do it too!"

"What?"

"The pepper!" She gulps some more. Milk runs down her chin, and she uses the back of her hand to wipe it off. "Eat it!"

"But..."

"Don't make me suffer alone!"

So I do it. For my sister. Before I can chicken out, I pick up a Carolina Reaper and put it in my mouth. I close my eyes and chew, already dreading the moment the heat kicks in and my mouth, tongue, and throat catch fire.

I swallow.

But...

Nothing happens.

My mouth just tastes peppery—the heat must be on a delay.

Then I hear laughing.

I open one eye, then the other.

Allie's holding her phone up and videoing me.

"Milk?" she asks, and hands me the carton.

"But it's not...it's not hot."

"No. But it *is* hilarious. You should totally see your face right now. Actually, here." She hands me the phone. "You can."

I roll my eyes. "I knew you would never get the Carolina Reaper."

"Maybe one day. Perhaps I need to start taking chances." Allie shrugs. "But I can't change everything at once."

CHAPTER 32

Jesse gets home after I've gone to sleep. Or, at least, after I've gone to his room and *pretended* to be asleep in his extra bunk.

He doesn't turn the light on when he comes in, but I hear him. I peek as he puts his shoes in his closet and then leaves the room with something in his hands. When he comes back a few minutes later, he's in his pajamas. He steps closer to me.

"Milo?" he whispers so quietly that I wonder if he really said my name or if I just imagined it.

I stay statue-still. He leans closer to me, like he knows I'm faking. He gives up and climbs into the bottom bunk.

It's too early in the morning when Allie comes into Jesse's room and flips on the light.

"Rise and shine, young men."

"Mom!" Jesse says. "It's the middle of the night."

"It's six a.m.," Allie says.

"Exactly." His voice is muffled by the pillow. "This is my off week from the meets. I want to sleep."

"Up, up, up." Allie claps with each word. "We're having a garage sale. Milo, you and Jesse need to put up signs while I pull stuff out."

As her brother, I want to tell her no and her idea is dumb, but she's using her I'm-an-adult-you-are-not tone, so I say okay and brush my teeth.

Once I'm dressed, I go into the living room. Jesse's already there, writing "GARAGE SALE" on a poster. Allie hands me a marker and tells me to do the same.

"If we planned this stuff, it would be better," Jesse tells his mom. "This isn't the right type of cardboard. Plus, we don't even have anything organized to sell."

"Lighten up, Jesse," she says. "It doesn't have to be perfect."

I snort before I can stop myself. Jesse glares, and I refocus on the signs.

Jesse and I finish the posters and, per Allie's instructions, we set out to tape them to street signs and light posts. We go in opposite directions, like magnets repelling each other.

I get back to the house first. While Jesse and I were gone, Allie set up three tables in the driveway. Now she's hauling boxes out of the garage. A car passes by and slows down as if the driver is checking out the invisible merchandise.

"Come on, slowpoke! I need help," she calls out to me. I jog up the driveway and grab a huge box. Allie tells me to open it and put the stuff inside onto the table.

The box is full of shoes. I find a brown leather loafer on the top and dig through the rest to find the match. I don't clue in to what is happening until I wonder why Allie is selling men's shoes.

Then it hits me. This is Todd's stuff.

I stop and carefully place the shoe back in the box. "Allie, what are you doing?"

She doesn't stop to answer my question. She's still hauling stuff out. "I told you. It's a garage sale."

"But this is Todd's stuff."

She sets her box on a table and points at me. "Precisely why I don't need it."

"But . . . ," I start. I don't exactly know how to finish my sentence.

I don't have to because Jesse walks up the driveway and picks up a shirt from the table. "What are you doing? This is Dad's."

Allie comes over to him. She takes the shirt out of his hands and puts it back. "It was."

"So, what are you doing with it?" he says like he's accusing her of something.

"Jesse, I think it's time."

"Nope," he says, slinging a pair of jeans over his shoulder. He picks up a full box and takes a step back toward the house. "You can't sell this stuff."

"I can, sweetie, and I'm going to."

"Mom," Jesse says. "Please don't do this. Not right now."

"I talked about this last night with Milo," Allie says. I cringe when I hear my name. "Sometimes we need to let go. I've been thinking about this for a while, and there's no better time to start."

I take a step back and bump against a table. A belt falls on the ground.

Jesse turns toward me. "Really?" he says. "Thanks a lot."

"I didn't say it like that. I was talking about *me*. I didn't—"

He's gone before I can finish.

He slams the garage door so hard, it bounces open again. Allie stares at it.

A car on the street stops in front of the mailbox. "This where the sale is?" a guy asks as he gets out. " 'Cause the signs . . . and the tables . . ."

"Yes," Allie says. She clears her throat and wipes her cheeks with the back of her hand, then turns toward him.

"Yes, it is," she says much louder. "Sorry, we're getting a late start. I'm still pulling out boxes. You can go through them if you want. Or come back later."

The guy looks at her and then at me like he thinks we're tricking him. "Eh. Know what? I forgot my coffee. I'll grab a cup and be back."

Allie nods too enthusiastically. "Good. Great. Yes, do that."

She goes into her garage to get another box. And then another. And another. I stand there. Because, yes, she is technically my sister, but Jesse, among other things, is my (so what if it is ex–) best friend.

"Do I need to tell Mom and Dad that you wouldn't help me?" Allie snaps, definitely like a sister.

I glance up to Jesse's window.

Allie sniffs. "He'll be okay," she says. "And it's time. It's what he needs."

She wipes at her face again. "And I do too. You get that, right?"

I'm sorry, I think to Jesse. "Yes, I do."

CHAPTER 33

help my sister all day by unloading boxes, carrying stuff to cars, and—when Allie says she needs the garage sale to be over—by helping her take everything left to Goodwill.

Jesse stays away. I think he's in his room, but when Allie calls him down for pizza, he doesn't come.

"I'll get him," I say.

I knock on Jesse's door, but there's no answer. It's unlocked, so I go inside.

Jesse is sitting on the floor in the middle of ripped and crumpled paper.

"Can I come in?"

He doesn't answer.

I bend down and pick up some of the trash—it's a torn-up picture. I recognize Jesse Owen's jersey. This is from the poster Todd hung in Jesse's room.

"Jesse," I whisper. "What did you do?" My stomach squeezes.

"We're getting rid of our old stuff, right? You got rid of me. Mom's getting rid of Dad."

I pick up another scrap of the poster, smooth it out as best I can across my stomach, and stack it on the desk. The corners of the poster are still on the wall beneath thumbtacks. I leave them there.

"Your mom wanted me to get you. The pizza is here."

"Tell her I'm not hungry," he says. He gets up and climbs into his bed and curls into a ball.

"Okay. I'll let her know."

I leave to go downstairs but keep the door open behind me. I tell my sister that Jesse isn't coming. I ask if I can take pizza to him. She says if he wants to eat, he can come get it himself. I tell her, "Yes, ma'am."

Allie and I watch a movie. At least, I pretend to, but I can't concentrate. When it's over, I fake a yawn and say how tired I am. Around eleven, I stop by the kitchen and grab two pieces of pizza and wrap them in paper towels.

"Milo," Allie says before I get to the stairs, and I freeze.

"You going to bed?"

"Yeah. I'm super tired."

"Okay. Well, will you turn around and tell me good night so I know you're not mad at me too?"

There's nowhere to put the pizza. I'm caught. I turn around slowly. "Good night?"

Allie crosses her arms. "So you're just ignoring what I said, then?"

I can't look at her. "I'm sorry. I'll put it back."

"No, don't. Jesse's lucky to have you. We both are." My sister stands up and gives me a one-armed hug so she doesn't squash the pizza. "Now, we're both going to pretend I didn't see you sneak this to him. Okay?"

I nod.

"Okay. Good night."

When I get to Jesse's room, his back is to me, but he's still awake. I set the pizza on the nightstand and climb up to the top bunk.

★ ★ ★

It's midnight and I can't sleep.

Based on his breathing, I'm guessing Jesse can't either.

Into the dark, I say, "Are you okay?"

Jesse does not answer.

"I didn't tell her to sell your dad's stuff."

Still nothing.

Maybe he *is* asleep.

"I always thought I was going to break a record and everything would be worth it. But now I know that's not true. That's all I told her I swear."

"I hate that I'm so jealous of the records," he says.

I snort.

"Stop laughing at me."

"I'm not. It's just—you're the perfect one. There's nothing for you to be jealous of."

"I'm not perfect. Stop saying that!" he snaps. Neither of us speak. Then he breaks the silence. "I miss my dad."

"I know," I say.

"He had bad breath."

"What?"

The bed shakes. I think Jesse's sitting up.

"Don't you remember? He drank coffee and when he talked to us, we wouldn't breathe out of our noses."

I don't think Jesse's done talking. I stare at the light patterns on the ceiling. The door is cracked, and there's a slash of light coming in from the hallway.

"He got really irritated sometimes," Jesse says. His voice is normal at first. "He'd yell. Once, when I left my Bob the Builder stuff out, he tripped on it. He got so mad at me.

"And he forgot *everything*." Jesse's voice is louder now. Higher. Like he's forcing out the words. "He forgot where he put his keys. He forgot when I had soccer games. Once, when I was four, he forgot to pick me up from preschool. Mom was so mad. The day he died"— his voice shakes—"he forgot his reflective vest. It was hanging on the hook at our house. Maybe if he'd worn it, the truck would have seen him. Maybe it wouldn't have hit him, and he'd be here now. I think about that every day. Sometimes I hate him for it. If *he* tried harder, if he'd been more perfect, maybe he wouldn't have died. But he doesn't get a do-over."

"I'm so sorry."

"And I really wish," he says, his voice cracking, "that I didn't tear my poster."

"I know."

I don't say anything else. There's nothing I can do to help right now. But at least he knows I'm there.

CHAPTER 34

My parents get home around lunch on Sunday. According to Guinness, the previous record for most people howling was 803. The new record is now 947. It could have been 949, but my parents missed their connecting flight and got to the attempt right after the record was set. Still, they got there in time to get a souvenir and brought me a T-shirt with a wolf on it. There's a speech bubble coming out of the wolf's mouth that says, "Howl do you like me now?"

First thing on Monday, Dad says, "We'll take you to school today. Want to ask Jesse if he wants a ride too?"

I pick up my phone, but I don't text him. I wait a

few minutes and say, "Jesse wants us to go ahead without him."

When we get to school, instead of dropping me off, my parents park and get out of the car.

"You don't have to walk me inside."

"Don't worry, we're not." Mom smiles. "We need to talk with your principal."

"What?"

"Relax, Milo. It's a good thing."

It is most definitely *not* a good thing. As soon as my parents go in there, Mr. Amondo will tell them that I ratted them out.

"I heard he was going to be out of town today."

"We'll stop by and see," Dad says.

"And Monday mornings are super busy in the office," I add.

"Milo," Mom says. "It's almost like you don't want us to talk to him."

"It's not that. I just don't want to get on his bad side."

"I promise we'll behave," Dad says as he lifts a cardboard box out of the trunk. "We won't mention your name at all. He won't even know we're related." They start going up the steps to the school, leaving me on the sidewalk.

"See you this afternoon, sweetie," Mom says.

I go to first period and sit down. Right now, my parents are probably figuring out what I did.

Brandon comes in and stops by my desk.

"Rematch today? After school at my house."

I nod. Good plan. I'll stay away from my house for as long as possible.

And actually, since Brandon's parents are never there, maybe I'll move in and nobody will even notice.

I close my eyes and pretend I'm in the principal's office with my parents right now. I wish I knew what was happening.

Dread sits on my shoulders like a fat parrot.

"Good morning," Mrs. Docet says. "I hope you had a great weekend. I plan on having a great week. Take out a piece of paper, add the heading, and number to ten. No better way to start the week than with a quiz."

This might be the worst day ever.

I add my name at the top of a blank sheet and then glance up at the date.

Oh no. Oh no. Oh no.

How did I forget this was coming? No wonder Jesse flipped out this weekend. Today is the anniversary of Todd's death.

Five years ago, we were sitting in class, clueless. The lady in the front office called Jesse's name and then mine over the loudspeaker. Like innocent, dumb little kids do, we bounced out of class, thankful to miss the treachery of second grade.

"Boys," said the counselor in a cotton-candy tone. "Your parents are here to take you home."

The plan, I found out later, was for us to go to Allie's house. There, my sister, mom, and dad would explain everything.

But that's not how it happened.

Jesse and I were signed out of school. As we walked down the steps out front, Allie stopped, collapsed to her knees, and threw up. My mom and dad ran to her. Jesse ran back in school to get help. I froze.

The school secretary and the principal hurried outside. They told us about Todd right there on the sidewalk. Between the four adults, they managed to get my sister to the car.

The whole way home, Jesse rocked back and forth and said, "We'll be okay. We'll be okay."

I was worthless. I bawled—full-on snot and moans. But when I finally dried up, I promised myself I'd make it up to Jesse. I turned worthless when he needed me most, and that would *never* happen again. Which is why I went after Brandon. And why four years ago I decided Jesse should not spend the first anniversary of Todd's death in school. It became a tradition.

Our parents have always written notes to excuse our absences; they've driven us to the movies or to the arcade, or, like last year, to both places because we figured out my sister and my parents would agree to whatever we asked. And, yeah, of course we knew we got something good because something so very bad had happened. But still, it made it a little better.

Today is the first time since the accident that we are here, sitting in class on the anniversary.

Even if Jesse and I are not really talking—even if we never talk again—I need to fix this.

Maybe my parents are still in the office and I can catch them.

I grab a trash can on the way to the teacher's desk. When I have Mrs. Docet's attention, I force a gag. This is a trick Jesse and I both perfected through practice, but we haven't used since fourth grade. "I think I'm going to be sick. I need to call my mom."

My teacher doesn't ask any questions. She just scribbles something unreadable on a sticky note and says to take the trash can with me.

When I get to the clinic, the nurse takes my temperature with the ear thermometer. Of course, it shows I don't have a fever, but I tell her because of the impending vomit and all, I should probably call my parents.

"Hello?" Mom says, answering her cell phone on the second ring.

"Mom, it's me."

"Milo? What is it? What's wrong?" Her voice is high. She's worried.

I want to tell her I'm okay, but I don't want to blow my cover. "Are you still here?"

"No. We're almost home. Are you sick?"

"I'm here in the nurse's office." I pause so she'll get the message. "It's today. I'm sick *today*."

"Okay," she says. "So I need to come get you?"

"Yes," I say. "But there's more." I just need to remind her about today, and she'll understand.

The nurse gets up from her chair. I'm hoping she'll leave, but instead she grabs a disinfectant cloth to wipe the plastic cot next to mine. When she washes her hands,

I use the noise of the water to rush out an explanation. "You need to get Jesse and me."

"Huh?" Mom says right as the water turns off, and I lose my chance to say it again.

"Five. Years," I say slowly.

The nurse stands straighter and turns an ear toward me. Now she's listening.

Mom sighs. "I know, Milo."

I clear my throat to make the shake in my words go away. "And we're at school."

"I'm aware of that as well."

"But we shouldn't be." The nurse completely turns to face me now.

"Milo, your sister already said no. And we're going to listen to her."

"Why didn't anybody tell me?"

"I'd assumed Jesse did."

"No!" I say. Now I really do feel sick.

"But we can still do something after school if you want," she says, her voice softer.

I swallow hard to try to smooth out the lump in my throat. "Whatever," I say.

"Milo," she says quietly. "Everything will be fine."

"Okay."

"Can you go back to class?"

"Yes," I answer.

We say goodbye, and I tell the nurse my mom thought I should stick it out. I walk back with an empty trash can and a signed pass.

When I'm in my chair, Jesse glances at me and I give him a head nod. Because, if nothing else, he needs to know I remember.

He nods back at me. A silent salute to Todd.

★ ★ ★

"You okay?" I ask Jesse in language arts.

He shrugs. "Yeah. Just...you know."

"Yeah."

I try to think of something else to add, but the past weeks of silent treatment make talking now seem too forced. I don't say anything else for the rest of the class.

"So," Jesse says right before the bell in Computer. "Mom said Nina and Pops missed another record."

I roll my eyes. "Yes. But they gave me this." I lean back so he can see my wolf shirt.

He smiles. "At least the swag was good."

After class we walk together in the hallway. I'm careful not to speed up or slow down—I don't want to be the one to break away.

"Hey," he says when we walk into the cafeteria. "I know the stuff that happened this weekend wasn't your fault."

"Yeah? Thanks."

We wind up at Jesse's table.

I'll sit here. Just for today.

Jason, Justin, and Luke don't say a word. At all. Like it is painfully obvious everybody is watching us and waiting for something to happen. I guess they've noticed over the past several weeks that MiloandJesse have had big spaces between them.

"Break any records lately?" Jason finally says.

Before I can answer, Jesse, in a burst of imperfection, says, "Shut up, man."

CHAPTER 35

Jesse catches up with me after the last bell. Our school is shaped like a square, with the lockers lining the perimeter. Instead of taking the shortest route, I use the other three hallways to give us extra time.

I shove my books in my locker and kneel down to stuff my binder into my bag.

"So," I say after I stand up. "I'm meeting Brandon after school."

Jesse shrugs. "Okay." He walks with me.

Brandon is waiting at the flagpole. "Good to see the two of you stuck together again. You coming to tell me you're too busy to hang out today, Record Breaker?"

I ignore the jab. "Maybe we can all do something?"
Jesse shrugs.

Hunter's Jeep pulls up to the curb and he honks.

Brandon shakes his head. "Nah. I'll catch you later.
I don't think my house is big enough for the three of us
together."

"Okay." I'm about to say we can go to my house, but
then I picture Brandon inside studying the Toilet Paper
Tower, and I shut my mouth.

"Nobody's allowed over when my mom's not home,"
Jesse says, "or I'd offer."

Brandon narrows his eyes at Jesse. "No, you wouldn't."

Jesse shrugs. "Maybe you're right."

"You know what?" Brandon says. "I think I'm busy
today."

Hunter pulls up in front of the school and honks for
way too long.

"No, you're not," I say. "Let's just go somewhere
else."

"He says he can't come," Jesse says. "Let him go."

"Don't worry, Record Breaker." He glares at Jesse.
"Go back to your little anthill without me."

"Are you calling me short or something?" Jesse says.

"Because I've heard all the jokes before, and usually they're better."

"Whatever." Brandon jogs to his brother's Jeep and opens the door. He throws his backpack on the floorboard of the car and climbs inside.

Jesse and I stand there and watch him ride away. "He wasn't calling you short."

"Then what was that all about?"

I start to tell Jesse about the ants and the grasshopper, but I don't think he'd get it. Not yet anyway. And it feels like I'd be talking bad about a friend.

"Nothing," I say. "Never mind. My house?"

CHAPTER 36

Jesse comes over, but he can't stay long because he's going to the batting cages with Jason. Maybe I'm the only one who thought Uncle Todd should be remembered today. Or maybe Jesse made plans because he couldn't count on me anymore.

I'm not sure what to do once he leaves. Mom's still in her office, and Dad's not home yet. I'd get on the Guinness site, but I realize there's no reason for that anymore.

I knock on Mom's office door and tell her I'm going on a walk. She reminds me to take my phone and to be home by six for dinner.

I don't know where I'm going. Or maybe I do.

I haven't ever been to Brandon's front door. We've always gone in through the garage. Some long, chime-y song plays when I ring the doorbell.

"What do you want?" Hunter says. I whip around, but nobody is there.

"I'm on a speaker, dummy," Hunter says. "I can see you."

"Oh. Um." I lean toward the doorbell. "Is Brandon there?"

"I can see up your nostrils. You have boogers."

I stand up and fight the urge to wipe my nose.

"Brandon's not here."

I don't believe him. But I don't know if he's lying because he hates me or because Brandon told him to. "Thanks."

"Welcome. And don't come back now, ya hear."

Turns out free time is overrated. I don't have the records to attempt, or Brandon or Jesse to hang out with.

On the way back home, I stop by my old elementary school and sit on the swings. I miss it here. But I'm glad it's all different too. I don't want to go backward.

CHAPTER 37

need you to do something for me," I tell Jesse on the way to school the next day. "But you're not going to like it."

"Okay?" Jesse says.

"You need to be friends with Brandon."

"What are you talking about?"

"We're all going to hang out."

"I don't trust that guy."

"Yeah. I know. He doesn't trust you either."

Jesse stops and looks at me like I'm crazy.

I shrug. "You both have good reasons."

Jesse closes his eyes, shakes his head, and then starts walking toward school again. "Just because you've decided to change everything doesn't mean we all have to."

"I'm not asking you to change everything—just the things that need changing."

"Whatever," Jesse says, and then walks five feet in front of me the rest of the way to school.

Since Jesse won't speak to me during first, third, or fourth period, it's not a hard decision to sit with Brandon at lunch.

"Hey," I tell him. "You're coming over after school today, okay?"

"Is Jesse coming too?"

"Not sure yet."

He crumples an empty bag of chips. "You know, I think I'm busy."

"I just need to warn you that you're going to see some things."

Brandon frowns. "What kind of things?"

"Hard to explain. Best to just wait and see."

"Are you manipulating me?"

"Yeah."

"Well done. You know, I'm more and more impressed with you every day, Record Breaker."

CHAPTER 38

Jesse got over himself and came to my house with Brandon. He stands there with his arms crossed like he's annoyed. Brandon, however, is not holding anything back. His mouth is open, and his eyes are huge. I pretend like I'm seeing my house for the first time just like Brandon is right now.

In front of the couch, there's a chest-high toothpick sculpture. My parents attempted to create the Statue of Liberty, but it looks more like a hot-glue-and-toothpick blob. Paper planes cover the chairs and side tables—these are the leftovers from a recent failed attempt of farthest flight by a paper airplane. And blocking the TV is a floor-to-ceiling cup tower. My parents were not even close to breaking the record for stacking speed.

"What is all this?" Brandon whispers. He turns in a slow circle and doesn't wait for an answer. He walks over to the toothpick sculpture. He hovers his hand over it like he wants to touch it, but then pulls his fingers back.

"Please," Brandon says. "Show me everything."

"Have some pride," Jesse tells him.

I take Brandon to the kitchen. He studies jars of empty candy wrappers on the counter. When I open the drawers, he gasps. He picks up the dice and lets them flow through his hand like water.

Jesse rolls his eyes.

"This is...amazing." Brandon walks over to the Tower and pokes it with one finger.

"Be careful," Jesse snaps.

The Tower wobbles, but it doesn't fall.

Brandon points to the rubber-band-ball chairs tucked beneath the kitchen table. "Can I sit on one of those?"

I roll one out for him. "Go ahead."

He sits and bounces a couple of times. "Huh. They're a lot harder than I thought they'd be. Milo, why didn't you tell me about your house? It's...it's..." He gestures like he's having trouble coming up with the words.

"Odd? Insane?" I suggest.

"Zany," Jesse says.

Brandon and I turn toward him.

"What? It's a good and accurate description."

Brandon shakes his head, "No. It's *awesome*."

"Really," I say. "It's not."

"It is though. Like another dimension." Then Brandon's eyes get wider. "And it keeps getting better."

"Oh." Jesse freezes. "Oh no."

They are both looking past me.

I turn around because, really, what could be worse than what they've already seen?

The answer is: my parents. They are both standing there holding hands in front of us. And they are dressed up as cows.

"This is officially *amazing*," Brandon whispers.

CHAPTER 39

I'm in awe too—but not in a good way. More like the way where it feels like my brain's been Tasered.

"So," Mom says. "What do you think?"

My parents wait for an answer as they show off their fuzzy, one-piece, head-to-toe cow costumes—complete with dangling udders. Their faces are painted white with black spots.

"Mom," I say slowly and clearly. "Did you notice we have company? This is Brandon."

There's a high-pitched hyena-type sound. Brandon slaps his hand over his mouth. "Sorry," he says.

"Hi, Brandon," Mom says, and waves to him. Then holds out her arms and spins. "Aren't they great!"

"They are," Brandon says. "So, *so* great."

"And aren't you going to ask why we have them on?" Dad says.

I swallow hard. "Mom. Dad. Why do you have those on?"

"For a record attempt!" Mom says. "And guess what? This time you definitely get to join us!"

"And," Dad adds, "all your friends will get to do it too. Because we're doing it at your school. We pitched the idea to your principal, and he *loved* it."

"I wouldn't say he loved it," Mom says.

Dad waves his hand. "Well, he agreed."

Mom smiles so big the spots painted on her face crinkle. "Yes, he agreed."

Dad tugs at the neck of the costume. It makes the bell around his neck jingle. "We'll set the record for the most humans dressed as farm animals who are reading. It's all going to work out perfectly! We almost can't fail this time."

His words break my stupor.

My brain processes this. My school. My parents dressed as cows. A new record.

"So very perfect," Brandon says.

"Everybody will be a cow?" Jesse asks.

"Oh, no! Any farm animal is fine," Mom answers.

In another room, the phone rings, and Dad leaves to answer it. My mother, in all her bovine glory, begins unloading the dishwasher.

"So cool," Brandon says. "I'm going to be a dog."

Jesse shakes his head. "Dogs aren't part of a farm."

"A sheepdog is."

"When's the last time you sang about a sheepdog in 'Old MacDonald'?"

"When's the last time you sang 'Old MacDonald'?"

I cover my eyes with my hands. "Are you two kidding me right now?"

Mom frowns at me. "Milo. Be nice to your friends."

"*Sorry*," I say, glaring at both of them. "So. Farm animals?"

Mom hangs the dish towel on the hook. "Right. Store-bought or homemade. The record to beat is five hundred sixty-four people. Think we can do it?"

"I think the real question is, *should* we do it?"

"Milo, this will be your official win. We've worked it all out." Mom wipes her cheek with the back of her hand. One of the spots streak. "Whew! This thing is hotter than I thought it'd be."

"Yeah," I say. "You should probably go change."

The second she's gone, Brandon covers his face with his hands. "I can't," he says, his shoulders shaking. "I literally cannot." He wipes his eyes. "We are never going to my house again."

"Shut up!" Jesse says. "She's going to hear you."

"Okay." He squeezes his eyes together. "Okay. I'm going to stop laughing," he says. "Any second. I will stop."

He doesn't stop.

Ignoring him, I turn to Jesse. "What am I going to do?"

"Obviously," Brandon says, snickering. "You're going to have to mooooo-ove."

"You're so frustrating," Jesse tells him.

"Wait! I've got a great idea!" Brandon says.

I don't want to ask him. I shouldn't ask him, but still, I say, "What is it?"

He leans forward. "Are you listening?"

Jesse and I both nod.

"First, we brainstorm the perfect plan. And then..."

He pauses. "Then?" Jesse asks.

"Then we take that plan and *milk* it for all it's worth."

Jesse laughs at that. When I glare at him, he says, "Sorry. But that was funny."

CHAPTER 40

It's too bad Guinness has declared some attempts as unsafe. Otherwise, I might be able to complete the record for most hours without sleep.

I pull out my phone and am almost tempted to go on the Guinness website. Instead, I start a group text with Jesse and Brandon.

Me: Anybody awake?

Jesse: Phone just buzzed. So I am now.

Me: Can't sleep.

Brandon: Try counting sheep? Might be some in your living room.

Jesse: You should consider blocking him.

Brandon: Just being helpful.

Me: :/

Jesse: You know, maybe this isn't so bad. Maybe this really is your chance to get a world record???

Me: Your mom's costume got here after you left.

Brandon: Is that a yo' momma joke?

Me: Nope. Allie's costume is sitting in the living room as we type.

Jesse: Still though. There are worse things that could happen.

Brandon: Is he serious right now?

Brandon: J, u serious right now?

Jesse: Just saying. In the grand scheme of things...

Brandon: That isn't what we are talking about. At all.

Me: Going to bed

Brandon: Early bird gets the worm

Brandon: Sleep tight. Don't let the bedbugs bite

Brandon: See ya later, alligator

Brandon: After while, crocodile

Jesse: Officially turning my phone off now

★ ★ ★

Both Jesse and Brandon have promised not to say a word about this to anybody. At lunch we find our own table so we can talk. At least, that's my excuse for why we have to sit alone. Really, I don't trust either of them to stay quiet.

"I just can't believe," Brandon says, "you've done this your entire life and haven't broken a record. I'm just fully appreciating this all. I mean, fail after fail after fail."

Jesse gives Brandon a deserved are-you-kidding-me look.

"You just kept going. That many losses. Can you even imagine?"

"Yes." I glare at him. "I can."

"Wait." Brandon sits up. "What if you could win for losing? Then you'd have the record and you wouldn't have to do another. And your parents wouldn't unleash themselves upon the school." He holds his hands up. "I solved everything. I'm a genius."

I rub my face. "Won't work. There are rules. You have to be able to measure the attempts."

"Do you know how many attempts you've made?" Jesse asks.

"Yeah. They're in Mom's office. But there's no way to prove we've actually *tried* to break the record. Like maybe the goal was to fail."

"Makes sense. I mean, I bet they don't believe anybody could even accidentally be so bad at so much."

"What now?" Jesse asks.

"Give up. Let it happen."

Brandon shakes his head. "Nah. Doesn't sound like something you'd do. Acceptance is not really your strong suit."

"Geez," Jesse says. "Just keep kicking him while he's down."

"I meant that as a compliment. Plus, now I'm working with you instead of against you. And I happen to be the master of"—he pauses and smirks—"sabotage."

"Whatever," Jesse says as he shoves his trash in a bag.

"Please refer to my most recent work: the Kangaroo Milo."

"Photoshopping does not make you the master of anything."

"What about tanking Milo in math?"

"He did that himself."

"Did he now?" Brandon raises his eyebrows. "Because only one of us cares about our grades."

Jesse sits up straighter. "I don't believe you," he says.

"Yes, you do," Brandon says. "Which is also another example. You don't want to like me. But still, you're impressed. You're thinking it's possible I'm an evil genius."

Jesse nods. "Yeah, but I'd leave the genius part out."

"Remember," I say to Jesse. "We're all friends now."

Brandon leans his chair back onto two legs. "Yup. Friends who will, together, master the art of"—he looks around—"*sabotage*."

Jesse's jaw clenches.

"See?" Brandon points to Jesse. "I just mastered you. Now you're not thinking clearly and I can control you."

"No, you can't," Jesse snaps.

"Or did I just succeed?" Brandon crosses his arms.

"So, then, what do we do next?" I ask. "How do we stop the record attempt?"

"All we have to do is figure out why all the past records didn't work and do that."

Jesse frowns. "This is totally going to fail." He looks at me. "You sure about this?"

"No. But unfortunately it's the best we've got."

"Aww!" Brandon says. "Pretty sure that's the exact same thing my parents say about me."

CHAPTER 41

We've already had the Fruity Pebbles and now we're in my room. Brandon's at my desk, Jesse's in the beanbag chair, and I'm on the floor.

"You're both here because I know I can count on you," I say, and look Brandon in the eye and then Jesse.

Jesse's face turns red.

I decide not to bring up when Jesse sold me out to the entire seventh grade. We're past that now. I trust him. Mostly.

"What you are about to see will stay between us. You will not talk about this unless absolutely necessary."

Brandon nods. "I probably swear to that."

"You mean solemnly," Jesse says.

"No, I don't."

My parents keep a file cabinet *full* of attempt info. The plan is to study it and to replicate the failures. This way we know it'll work. And we won't get caught because it'll be believable.

"So, first, we've got to figure out how to get the records. How do we get my mom out of the office?"

"Great." Brandon rubs his hands together. "Where's the fire alarm?"

"If you set off the fire alarm at a house, you don't leave." Jesse puts his hands behind his head. "You go figure out what is wrong."

"Duh," Brandon says. "That's why we're going to start a small fire. It'll create a distraction."

Jesse closes his eyes and shakes his head.

"I said a *small* fire. At least I have a plan."

"So do I." Jesse gets up and leaves the room. We follow him.

"Hi, Nina," he says when he gets to the office.

She looks up and sees us. "Hey, guys. What's new?"

"Hi, Mrs. Moss." Brandon picks up the plaster cast Mom made when she attempted to grow the longest fingernails. He sets that down and immediately picks up a tiny glass bottle from the desk. He rolls it over in his hand, and all the minuscule pieces clatter inside. "Is this supposed to be a ship?"

"The world's smallest inside a bottle," I say.

"I'm still working on that project for school. Milo said you've saved stuff about the past records. I was going to see if I could look at some of it," Jesse says.

"Of course." Mom scoots her chair over to the file cabinet. "How many do you want?"

"As many as I can look at."

Mom laughs. "That would take days. How about I give you a stack and I'll switch those out as soon as you're done."

"Thanks, Nina," Jesse says, and Mom loads him up.

Back in my room, we sort the stack of attempts into categories of Food, Crowd-related, Physical, Skill, and Luck.

Some of the losses are no-brainers. Like, in the Food category, for example. Turns out Mom, Dad, or I just physically can't eat seventy hot dogs or catch fifty-three marshmallows in our mouths in sixty seconds. Some of the fails are just bad luck. Like the time we went to the world's largest crawfish boil and figured out I had an allergy to shellfish. I didn't even eat the actual crawfish—just the potato it touched—but my eyes swelled shut and my whole body itched, and I had to go to the hospital for a shot.

Some fails, though, are just dumb. Like the one where we planned to be at the Elvis flash mob at the right day and time, but the completely wrong month. Or when we ran out of gas, not once or twice, but instead a whopping *five times.*

The shellfish allergy is our first inspiration. Though nobody's naturally allergic to cow costumes or horse heads, so we improvise.

"Three bottles of itching powder enough?" Brandon asks as he searches on the laptop.

I shrug. "No idea."

"You're the diabolical one," Jesse says. "Why are you asking us?"

"It's Master of Sabotage," Brandon corrects. "Plus, you are my accomplices. And my students."

Jesse shifts in the beanbag chair but doesn't say anything.

Brandon pushes the desk and wheels back from the

computer. "All set. Three bottles of itching powder and one siphon pump for gas will be here in two days. That way you can have car trouble whenever you need to."

"Thanks, man. I promise to pay you back," I say.

"Don't worry about it. It's not my money. It's my parents'."

"Won't they notice?"

"Nope. They don't notice anything I do. And if they do, they don't care."

"That's kind of messed up," Jesse says.

"It is what it is. Some things you can't do anything about."

But some things, I hope, you can. Which is why we spend the rest of the night watching YouTube videos on how to siphon gas so we are ready to use the pump when it arrives.

CHAPTER 42

We're finally in town on a Saturday so my parents can go to one of Jesse's cross-country meets. They leave to get Allie at seven forty-five in the morning on Saturday. My parents think I'm still sleeping. I wouldn't mind seeing Jesse and Brandon run, but last night I told them I had too much homework and I wanted to get an early start. Really, I stay home because I have diabolical stuff to do.

Yesterday after school, I got the supplies we ordered from Brandon. The itching powder comes with tons of warning labels about how it could potentially cause irritation if it touches your skin. Duh. I hope it does.

I change into a long-sleeve shirt and pants and grab some gloves out of the garage. Cross-country meets are short. I've got thirty minutes max before my parents are back. I run into the first problem while I unpack the costumes. I have no idea which costume belongs to which person because they're all the same size. My only option is to contaminate all of them.

"Sabotage," I whisper to myself.

Two bottles would probably work for all the costumes, but I use all three to be thorough. When I'm done, I wrap the empty containers into grocery store bags, shove them in the middle of the trash, and take the entire bag out to the garage. The big door starts opening right as I step out the door. I sling the bag into the bigger container that holds everything until the day we take it out and run back inside, somehow slamming my middle finger in the door. The door pops back open.

There's no time to think about how much that hurts if I want to get away with my crime. I shut the door and run back to my room as I shake my hand to stop the throbbing.

"Milo?" Mom calls out from downstairs. "We're home."

Before I leave my room, I rub my head to mess up my hair. "Hey." I fake a yawn and stretch when I get to the kitchen. "Just got up."

"So much for getting your homework done," Dad says.

"Oh. Yeah," I say as I notice some powder on the floor. Gah! I'm so bad at this. Before my parents can notice, I walk over and spread it around with my foot. "How'd Jesse do?"

"Won," Dad says. "Gets those running genes from me."

Mom rolls her eyes. "Pretty sure that's from Todd's side of the family."

"Hey. I do marathons."

"But Todd actually won races," I say as I grab a piece of bread from the bag and shove it into my mouth.

"Big talk from the guy who slept in this morning. You know you have my genetics too, Milo. Maybe you should try out the running thing."

"No, thanks," I say as a tingle starts on the bottom of my big toe.

"Come on. It's a great way to set a record. You can run a marathon in a costume and it's basically a guaranteed win."

The tingle grows into a tickle. Then it's a full-blown itch.

"Honey!" Dad calls out to Mom. "I think I just thought of another record for our family to try. A marathon with the three of us in a joint costume!"

I rub my toe on the floor, but it doesn't help. I put all my weight on the itchiest spot and press down.

Ah. Sweet relief. At least I know the itching powder works.

"Great idea!" Mom says. "What costume are you thinking?"

I'm about to tell them both there will be no costume and no marathon because there will be no record, but I recognize the opportunity. "Maybe you should put on the cow costumes and jog around the block. You know, see how it goes."

"Great idea, Milo!" Dad pats me once on the back. "Family run tonight. Cattle attire required."

"Sounds great," Mom says. "We'll be like our own little herd."

★ ★ ★

The good news is I got out of the stampede when Allie invited Mom, Dad, and me over for pizza.

Except that my parents bring Allie her cow costume.

The itching powder is meant for Dad—Mom if necessary—but definitely not my sister.

When they give the box to my sister, I reach for it. "I'll take it for you." I can bring it straight to Jesse's room this way. Hide it in his closet or something.

"No, you eat. I'm just going to put it in my room."

"It's fine," I say. "Trust me."

"No," Allie says. "*You* trust *me*."

"Allie—"

"*Milo*," she mimics. "Stop being such a teenager. I've got this."

I clench my teeth, but I let my sister take it and I text Jesse.

Me: Where r u?

Jesse: Room.

Me: Your mom has a costume box. Find it. Hide it.

He doesn't text again, but he's downstairs about a minute after Allie comes back. He gives me a tiny nod.

CHAPTER 43

You know, I've been thinking," Brandon says. He, Jesse, and I are on the playground of our old elementary school. We stopped by on the way to my house. Brandon's sitting on the edge of the ball pit and holding a handful of pebbles. He's tossing the rocks back onto the ground one at a time. "When somebody grows out their fingernails for a record, how do they wipe?"

Jesse hits the tetherball from one of his hands to the other. "Seriously, man?"

"Ohhh, you're right. That's dumb. They'd just use the other hand."

"Gross." Jesse hits the tetherball hard so the rope wraps around the pole.

I go down the slide and stay at the bottom. "So. What's our next plan? Because I still haven't gotten my parents to put the costumes on again," I say.

"Why not?"

"I can't just be like, 'Hey, Mom and Dad, why don't you dress up as cows again?'"

"Sure you can," Brandon says. "If you're smart about it."

"Or you could just, you know, tell them to stop," Jesse says.

"I've tried."

"Like you've literally said, 'Mom. Dad. I do not want to do this anymore.'"

"Yup. And they said they understood. And then they talked to the principal and got him to agree to my public humiliation."

Jesse shrugs. "Ever think you should just go with it?"

Brandon throws a pebble at Jesse.

"Thanks, Brandon," I tell him.

He nods. "My pleasure."

"I may not have a choice if I don't figure something out."

Brandon opens his hand and lets the rest of the rocks fall to the ground. "Obviously you have to give up."

I roll my eyes. "I didn't say that."

"Good. Because I know what we are going to do next for...wait for it, *sabotage*."

"Great." Jesse sighs.

Brandon points to him. "You'll like this plan. Know why?"

Jesse shakes his head. "I don't think I want to."

"Because you, my friend, have a starring role."

CHAPTER 44

Jesse and I hate his idea. It took Brandon one day to convince me and then two more days to talk Jesse into doing it.

But nothing else has worked so far, and they're passing out flyers at school soon. Once that happens, there's nothing we can do to stop it.

Mom and Dad get packages in the mail every day. Pig snouts, chicken hats, and horse heads cover every surface of our living room. They stare at me with their unblinking plastic eyes whenever I walk through.

Our living room looks like a butcher shop. It smells like burnt popcorn and old tires; every opened box adds to the fumes of plastic and rubber.

It turns out though, Brandon, Jesse, and I aren't going to stop the record-setting embarrassment. Our principal will. At least, he will when we use his computer to send a letter to the counselor.

We meet up before school on Friday morning. Before we walk the rest of the way, Brandon hands me the flash drive.

"It's just," Jesse says for the hundredth time, "isn't hacking pretty serious?"

"We're not doing criminal-mastermind stuff. It's borrowing his email. And his name. And his authority. We just sneak into his office, copy a letter onto his computer, and send it to the counselor."

"And I really have to embarrass myself?" Jesse asks.

Brandon claps him on the back. "You most certainly do."

When the bell rings, as planned, neither Jesse nor Brandon are in their seats. I check my watch as I listen to the announcements.

Exactly seven minutes later, I tell Mrs. Docet I need to see the principal.

The teacher hesitates before she writes the pass, but she lets me go.

At the opposite end of the main hallway, Brandon

waits. He gives me a thumbs-up. Good. Brandon and Jesse's part of the plan worked. Mr. Amondo should be on his way to coaxing Jesse out of a fetal position in the upstairs boys' bathroom. This is where Brandon supposedly found him before school.

The light in Mr. Amondo's office is off, but the door is open. Acting like I have a reason to be there, I step inside and flip on the light. I shut the opaque glass door behind me.

The principal's office is directly across from the counselor's, and through the interior office window, I see Ms. Rogers sitting at her desk. She could look up any minute and catch me. So I close the blinds in the office. Go time.

Mr. Amondo's computer is completely black.

I wiggle the mouse. At first nothing happens, but then there's a static pop from the computer, and the monitor lights up. The home screen is full of icons, and my eyes are moving too fast to find the picture of the closed envelope that Brandon told me to look for. I take a deep breath and try again. This time I see it in the bottom left-hand corner of the screen. I move the arrow to the icon, click, and I'm in.

My hands shake as I take the flash drive out of my

pocket. The USB outlet on the front of the computer tower is like a tiny mouth waiting for its electronic meal. When I feed it the drive, a small spinning wheel appears on the computer screen for a few seconds, and then a white box opens to show a single file: Principal.

I double click on the file. The letter we wrote to the counselor opens.

Dear Ms. Rogers:

I am concerned about the record attempt scheduled at our school. It is my job to protect the well-being of our students. I fear this event will harm the budding self-esteem of Milo Moss as well as make him the target of extreme ridicule. Also, the Moss family has a history of failure, and many of the students may not be able to handle this level of disappointment. Therefore, the record attempt is not in the best interests of our students. Because of this, I am canceling the event. Please contact the Moss family and inform them. Immediately.

Best Regards,
Mr. Amondo

In the hallway, a door opens. My heart tries to beat itself out of my chest.

After three deep breaths, I crack the door. Across the hall, Ms. Rogers's office is now empty and the lights are off.

She's gone. I'm not getting caught. We're totally getting away with this.

I highlight the words of the letter, click copy, and paste it to a blank email. When I start typing the counselor's email address, the computer finishes it for me. This is so easy; it's going to work.

I press Send.

Somewhere outside the office, I hear Jesse.

"Wait," he says. "I don't think we need to go to *your office*. I think I just need to stay here a minute. Right here." Louder, he adds. "In this chair."

I'm already at the door when I remember the flash drive. I rush back over to the computer, yank it out, and shove the evidence in my pocket.

When I barely crack the door open, I see Jesse sitting in a chair and hugging a trash can on his lap. He glances my way and his entire body tenses. "It's coming!" He dry heaves into the trash can. It's very convincing.

"Uh." Mr. Amondo takes a step back. He turns his head—thankfully in the direction opposite of me. I tumble out of his office.

"I'm just"—Jesse perfects another gag—"very emotional right now, I guess."

Then Jesse sees me. "Oh," he says, setting the trash can down and using the back of a shaking hand to wipe his mouth. "Oh, good. Milo's here." His voice is quieter now. Weaker. He holds a hand out to me. "Milo. Come here. I need you. I just got sick."

Mr. Amondo looks into the trash can and frowns. "I don't—"

"I feel awful," Jesse says. He stands and puts his arm around my shoulders like his legs might give out.

I elbow him in the ribs.

He stands up straighter. "Though I'm better now that my family is here."

I manage to keep my voice steady as I say, "Come on. I'll take care of you, buddy."

Mr. Amondo doesn't stop us.

"Congratulations," I whisper to Jesse as I guide him into the hallway.

"For what? Did I pull it off?"

"Sort of. But, even more impressive, I think this is the first time you've managed to get an adult to dislike you."

CHAPTER 45

I want to celebrate and mentally replay the whole scheme with Brandon and Jesse after school, but I go home alone instead.

My parents may be devastated or angry or confused. And I'll have to hide my relief. Hopefully I'm a better actor than Jesse.

"Hi, honey," Mom says when I walk into the living room. She's brushing the mane of one of the horse heads. She sets down the comb, picks up the mask, and turns it around in her hands. "Perfect." She sets it into a box and then picks up the comb again and starts on the next one.

"So, um. What's going on?"

"Just getting stuff ready."

I set my bag down. This is worse than I thought. She's gone crazy.

"For what?"

"The counselor called. Dad and I are going up for a meeting in a bit. Must be important if the principal wants to meet on a Friday afternoon, huh? Anyway, I thought I'd go ahead and take up the costumes we got for the administrators." Mom pauses to look at me. "You okay, Milo? You don't look so good."

"I'm fine." Except, I don't know if that's true. I pull out my phone as I back out of the room. "But I have homework. Bye."

In the safety of the hallway, I text Jesse and Brandon.

Me: !!!! Parents have a meeting at the school. Today!

Jesse: Weird.

Me: I think it worked.

Brandon: Don't let them go!!!

Me: What? Why?

I stare at the screen waiting for a text, so when the phone rings in my hand, I jump. Brandon's name is on the screen.

"Hello?"

"Sabotage!" Brandon says. "Do not let them go. Your parents will persuade them to do the records. In five minutes it'll be sorted out."

My phone beeps, and I look at the screen. "Hold on. Jesse's calling. I'll put him on too."

"They'll know what we did!" Jesse says when I answer.

I pull the phone away from my ear. "Hold on." I press the Merge Calls button. "Everybody's here."

"What are we gonna do?" Jesse's still yelling.

"Well," Brandon says. "You're going to freak out. Obviously. And Milo's going to stop the meeting."

"How?"

"You're going to have car trouble. Do you remember the YouTube videos we watched? You've trained for this, Milo. Go make us proud."

CHAPTER 46

It's done. Everything worked just like the tutorial said.

The gas is now out of the car and in a bright red container in our side yard.

"Milo," Mom calls from the front door.

I jog over. "Hey." Fumes of gasoline come off my fingers, so I shove my hands in my pockets.

"I need to go. Would you help me with these boxes?"

"Yeah." I take the one from her hand and head to the car.

"Dad is meeting me at the school. He's coming from work. We'll grab dinner on the way home for us," Mom says as she gets in the car.

Wait. How could I have forgotten about Dad? Of course he'd want to meet with them too. I've got to be there.

"Mom. Wait." I rush toward the car. "Can I come too?"

She stops and tilts her head to think. "I don't see why you couldn't."

I don't know if I'm hoping the siphoning worked or if I'm hoping it didn't.

I get in the car, hold my breath, and squeeze my eyes shut.

Mom turns the key. The car fires right up. I think it's laughing at me.

I'm so seriously bad at everything I do. I look out the side window and focus on the car coming down the street.

Mom reverses out of the driveway.

And then...the engine dies.

Just like that.

The car shuts down when we are halfway out onto the street.

I sit up in my seat. "What happened?"

Mom's studying all the dials. "I don't know. The car just stopped."

So, wait. I did it?

Then—*BAM*—something hits us. At first I think it's the feeling of victory. But then, outside the window, the world moves.

Everything feels like it's in slow motion: Mom's confused expression, the view changing slowly from my house, to the side yard, to the street, and then the realization that another car has hit ours.

When we stop moving, Mom says, "Oh my gosh. Milo. Are you okay?"

"Yeah," I say. Then I clear my throat. "Yeah. I think so. Are you?"

She pauses to check. She rubs her arm. "I think I hit my shoulder. But I'm fine."

Suddenly my door opens and somebody is reaching in. "Oh my gosh, oh my gosh, oh my gosh. Please tell me you're okay. I'm sorry. I'm so sorry!"

I let somebody else's hands pull me out. It's a kid. Older than me, but not an adult.

"I just looked down for a minute. I swear."

Mom comes over to my side right as the dude starts crying.

"What can I do?" she says. "Are you hurt?"

"No." The guy shakes his head. "But I ran into you. I'm so sorry."

Mom hugs him. "What's your name, sweetie? Are you sure you're okay? Is there somebody we need to call? You didn't mean to. It's okay. Our car stalled."

"I swear I just looked down for a second!"

Then I have the slowest realization of all: This is all my fault. I just caused this car wreck.

Mom makes the kid sit on our porch. She calls his parents and Dad and then two tow trucks.

"Guess we're not going anywhere tonight," Mom says as we watch our car get pulled away.

I can't look her in the eyes. "I guess we're not."

Mom puts her arm around me. When I look at her, she's crying. "I just keep thinking that if we were any farther out, the car would have run right into you."

"I'm so sorry," I whisper.

"Oh, Milo, this is not your fault." She kisses me on the head. "Let's go inside."

I let her lead me. I will do whatever she says.

I guess some things are more important than winning.

CHAPTER 47

When I come downstairs Saturday morning, every-thing is different. Literally. The house is clean. Too clean. The record-setting stuff is all gone.

Mom runs tape down the top of a box in front of her and then adds it to a stack of three others.

"What's going on?" I ask. "Where is everything? Where's Dad?"

"In the garage."

"But I don't understand. What's happening?" Our living room is...normal. There are no animal parts, no stacked cups. Even the half-done toothpick sculpture is missing.

"I'm just cleaning up a little," Mom says. "You hungry?"

The kitchen is different too. Only normal stuff like a toaster and a coffee maker sit on the counter. The Toilet Paper Tower no longer exists. Where could it have gone?

The rubber-band-ball chairs are the only record-breaking thing that's left.

"There he is," Dad says, walking in from the garage. "The man of the hour!"

"Got another one ready for you, honey," Mom calls from the living room.

He goes to the living room and comes back through the kitchen carrying a box. I follow him into the garage. One entire side is already packed full.

"What's in those?"

"Stuff we don't need anymore," Dad says. "Everything from our record breaking."

I'm afraid to ask more questions, but I have to get answers. "Why?"

"Help me get another box?" Dad asks.

I follow him back through the kitchen and into the living room.

"After you and your mom got hit yesterday, we had to ask ourselves some hard questions: What are we doing? Why are we doing it? And, even if we *can* do it, does that mean we should?"

"But we're totally fine."

He takes another load to the garage. "Yeah, but we got lucky. Sometimes when you want something so much you lose sight of reality."

"So, the attempts are over?" I ask.

"They are."

I guess I got what I wanted.

So why do I feel like this is the biggest fail I've ever had?

CHAPTER 48

"W hoa," Brandon says when we get to my house after school on Monday. "It looks so different in here."

"It does," I say. Over the weekend the transformation into normalcy was completed. Without the record-setting stuff, my living room is huge. And perfect. And maybe a little bit lonely.

"You really got your win this time," Jesse says as he sits on the couch.

"Everything is so…lame." Brandon frowns. "Where'd it all go?"

"Garage. My parents say they're getting rid of it soon."

"So what should we do now?" Jesse asks. "I could go for some Fruity Pebbles."

"I'm not really that hungry. We could watch TV or something, I guess." Actually, I wish they'd leave.

"We could go to my house," Brandon says.

"I think I just want to stay here." I add, "But you guys should go."

"We could play record-breaker roulette," Brandon says. "Open one of the boxes and do something with whatever we find."

"I don't really feel like doing anything." I sit in the chair. I can because there are no paper planes in it. "It's just, I thought it would feel different. Like, I'd be happy about it or something."

"Milo," Jesse says, and he cringes like he's sorry for his words before he even says them. "Have you ever considered that maybe it's not the records that's the problem?"

Brandon sits in the chair next to mine. "We could see who can spin around in these the fastest. Whoever pukes first loses."

I ignore Brandon. "Are you saying it's me?"

"I don't know. Maybe it is something to think about?"

"Are you guys going to start fighting again? Look.

Milo, would it help if we went back to being enemies? Might give you something to do."

Jesse raises his hand. "It'd help me."

I glare at Brandon. "Don't be a doofus."

Brandon shrugs. "I don't know. I'm just trying to help." He gets up and walks toward the kitchen.

"Where's he going?"

"I don't know."

When he comes back, he's wearing a huge plastic horse head. "Look what I found! I didn't even have to open a box. This was right on top." He pets the mane.

"Take that off," Jesse says.

"I challenge you both to the most hops on one foot while wearing this mask. And go!"

He starts jumping. The head flops around until it faces the wrong way.

"You look ridiculous," I say. Because he does.

"You'll never be able to beat me if you don't get out of that chair." His voice is muffled.

"I'm okay with that."

"You're lying." He stops. "Whew! Okay. Forty-six is the number to beat."

He takes off the mask and plops it onto Jesse's head. "Sorry it's wet. I sweat a lot."

"Gross!" Jesse throws it off.

Brandon picks up the mask, and he puts it on Jesse again.

"Are you going to get up?" Brandon asks.

Jesse says, "No."

"Okay. Then congratulate me. I'm the winner."

Jesse stands up, takes off the mask, and plops it backward onto Brandon's head. Then Jesse pushes him—just barely, a finger to the shoulder—but still, it works.

Brandon stumbles, and his leg hits on a chair. He reaches out to stop his momentum, but he falls on his butt.

Nobody moves at first. Then I look at Jesse, and he looks at me and we crack up.

I seriously can't even breathe. Jesse has tears running down his face.

"Oh, I've been waiting for this moment." Brandon is smiling as he takes off the mask. "Finally you're fighting back." He rubs his hands together. "It's on."

"Bring it," Jesse says.

"Thank goodness. I've been so bored without a rival."

CHAPTER 49

Jesse's right. The problem isn't the records. But the problem isn't necessarily me either.

The thing is, I've been failing all wrong.

On Tuesday I don't leave the house in my cow costume. Instead, I carry it in a big bag and wait until I'm a block from school to put it on. I hope I wiped out all the itching powder.

Maybe this public humiliation will show Mr. Amondo that I'm fully committed. Plus, can you really suspend a guy in a fuzzy cow costume?

I haven't even told Jesse or Brandon what I'm doing. But I did ask them to meet me in front of school five minutes before the bell. The stairs present a challenge, since I have limited vision with the mask on.

I waddle down the sidewalk wearing the extra thirty pounds. Even with sounds muffled, I can hear the random "Mooooo" when people see me.

Jesse and Brandon are waiting for me right where I asked. I wish I could see their expressions.

"Will you guys help me up the stairs?" I hold out my hands. "I can't see beneath my udder."

"That *is* you," Jesse says.

Brandon takes one of my arms and starts to pull. "Told you."

"What's happening?" asks a random kid as we all walk up.

"Just a delivery," Brandon says. "Haven't you ever wondered how they get the milk and burgers for lunch?"

"Both of you are killing me," Jesse says.

"You'll be fine," I yell through the mask. "Trust me. You've been through much worse."

Brandon and Jesse lead me to the principal's office. I tell them to leave me there and I promise to give them every detail later.

"There's something I need to tell you before you go

in there," Jesse says. But I don't have time to ask him what he wants to say.

"What is going on here?" Mr. Amondo asks. I can't see his face, but I can tell by his voice that he's not thrilled to have a cow in the office.

"Jesse." I put my fuzzy hoof on his shoulder. "It's going to have to wait."

I turn around. "Mr. Amondo? I need to talk to you."

The principal doesn't say a word. He leads me to his office and sits behind his desk.

"I'm not a real cow." I take off my oversized mask and set it at my feet. He's staring. Sort of like he's afraid. "Don't worry."

"You cannot wear that to school."

I shrug. "That's what I thought too. But here I am."

He reaches for his phone.

"Wait." I hold up a hoof. "Can I talk to you before you call my parents? Please? Because I want to tell you that I made a mistake."

"I can see that."

"No, not about this. This"—I gesture at the costume— "is awesome. I don't know what I was so afraid of."

"Detention, perhaps?"

"Anyway," I say before he continues down that trail.

I cringe as I say the next part. "I need to confess something. I wrote an email and sent it to Ms. Rogers's computer like it was from you. I said we should cancel the record attempt that my parents wanted to do here."

He nods. "Yes. I know."

"Wait. You know?"

"I do. I was assuming your parents had sent you here to apologize," Mr. Amondo says. He points to his ceiling at a sprinkler-looking thing. "Your parents didn't tell you we have it all on camera?"

Suddenly this cow onesie is superhot. And there's a place on my arm that tells me I definitely didn't wipe out all the itching powder. "No."

"When Ms. Rogers asked about an email I didn't send, the time stamp showed us exactly when to check the video feed in my office."

"Oh." This changes my mission. "Uh, am I in trouble?"

He frowns. "For the email or for your dress-code violation? Email-wise, I'm not sure. I called in the parents of the students involved. However, as I understand it, your family had some sort of car trouble. I spoke with Jesse's mother—your sister. She assured me it'd all be handled. I assumed it had."

I picture the boxes in the garage, as well as our now

normal, non-record-breaking house. "Actually, Mr. Amondo. Allie talked to them. They did handle it. I just didn't understand until now. I'm sorry. Really. About everything."

"Well," he says, straightening a picture on his desk. "Thank you, Mr. Moss."

"Hey, wait," I say without thinking. "Where's your Principal of the Year plaque?"

"Gone." He shrugs.

"Did they really come and take it away?"

He laughs. He actually looks nice. Friendly, even. "No. But I realized it was clouding my judgment. I lost sight of what really matters. But back to"—he gestures at me—"this cow situation. What is the plan here?"

"Mr. Amondo, I've messed up." I point to him with my hoof. "And I need your help to fix it."

"Mr. Moss, this has got to be the most creative attempt to get out of trouble I've ever seen. I'm intrigued."

"Does that mean you're in?"

The bell rings. I'm officially late to first period.

"Possibly. But for now, it means I'll listen."

CHAPTER 50

I am aware that *tons* of stuff can go wrong during a record attempt. So I study all the failures and know what I need to do differently.

Mr. Amondo gave me permission to use the parking lot of the school. All the teachers in the science department said they'd help too. I posted the future attempt to the online board. So far, we've gotten fifty-four RSVPs, and it's only been up for eight hours.

Brandon and Jesse help me make a spreadsheet. We list everything we need to make a liquid nitrogen volcano. Before dinner, I print the list and bring it downstairs. My parents are on the couch in our completely normal and totally uninteresting house.

"Mom. Dad. I need to talk to you." I stand where the coffee table used to be. "I need your help."

Dad looks up from his book. Mom closes her laptop.

"I know that you know what I did," I say.

Mom nods.

"Why am I not in trouble?"

Dad smiles. "Do you want to be? We can ground you if you want."

"No. But I do want help getting everything out of the garage."

"It's okay, Milo," Mom says. She stands up and hugs me.

I pull away from her. My nose burns. I rub it. "I want to tell you some stuff."

Mom pushes my hair off my forehead. "Okay."

"I thought a record-breaking win would show that I was somebody important. That it would make us—make me—matter."

"Milo," Dad says. He clears his throat. "You always matter."

"Parents always say stuff like that. I had to figure it out for myself. I did though. And guess what else I've figured out."

"What?" Mom asks.

I smile. "How to finally break a record."

Mom crosses her arms. "Milo—"

"*But* I'm also somebody who knows even if I don't, I'll be okay."

Mom hugs me again. This time Dad joins us. When he squeezes, my face squishes against Mom's shoulder.

"I still need your help though."

"Shh!" Dad says. "We're having a moment."

I give them another three seconds of family hugging.

"We're going to need your gigantic cake pan. This time it'll work perfectly."

"Milo." Dad steps back. "I've already tried making a gigantic oven. The fire department wrote me a ticket."

I shake my head. "Nope. It's going to be the top of our liquid nitrogen volcano. But I need you to figure out how we're going to build it."

Dad scratches his head. "You want me to engineer the structure of a gigantic volcano?"

"Yup."

"Yes," Dad says. "I will one hundred percent do that. I'm thinking a lattice infrastructure supported by crossbeams."

"Whatever you want."

"And, Mom, can you help me spread the news? Like promote it or whatever. We need people to bring stuff."

She makes her Concentration Face. "I can definitely get the word out. But first you've got to tell me, what are we doing?"

"We're going to use our failures to finally celebrate a win."

CHAPTER 51

The largest liquid nitrogen model volcano record was set by a "Trashcano" in 2017. Today we will shatter that record in the parking lot of our school.

Our volcano isn't made of trash though. It's made of, in Mom's words, experience.

Wrecked cars—including ours—make the structure of the volcano. The biggest cars are on the bottom, and the smallest on the top, so it's shaped like a mountain. A call to a junkyard supplied the necessary broken-down vehicles and a guy with the equipment to move them. He said he'd help us as long as he got credit in the interview we have with Channel 8 News.

For the past week, my family, Allie, Jesse, Brandon, and even Mr. Amondo have taken turns being at the volcano from four to eight o'clock every day. That's when people can bring stuff to add to the pile. Even when it rained for two days straight, people still showed up.

Yesterday when I was checking the pile, I saw Mr. Amondo pull something from his jacket and shove it through one of the glassless window frames of a crunched car. When he caught me looking he came over.

"You know I didn't tell you this earlier," he said, "but your sister really let me have it the other day. Said my students had real lives, real struggles outside the classroom and if I didn't understand that there was more at stake than grades and tests, then I didn't deserve my Principal of the Year plaque. I thought about it awhile and decided she was right. I took it down and you show up in my office with your scheme an hour later." He shook his head and laughed. "You've got quite the family. I can't decide if you all exhaust or inspire me."

"Could it be both?"

"Absolutely," he said, and squeezed my shoulder as he walked away.

When I went to see what he'd added to the pile, I

found a copy of a standardized test and his plaque with a sticky note that said, "Thanks for the reminder that the world's bigger than I'd made it."

★ ★ ★

Our volcano is beautiful. Participation trophies glitter in the sun. Snow skis and old guitars stick out of the side. Neckties sway when the wind blows. There's even a treadmill and a TV. Yesterday, a lady came in crying and dragging a wedding dress. She flung it on top of the pile. When she finished, she stepped back, brushed herself off, and whooped.

Mom, Dad, and I brought the rest of our record-breaking stuff this morning. I'm stuffing the last of the pig noses in random crevices when Jesse shows up carrying a huge box. "I need to talk to you about something." His face is pale. He looks sick.

He sets the box at his feet. Todd's jeans are folded and stacked on top. It's what Jesse took from the garage sale.

"Jesse, you don't have to give that stuff up."

He shakes his head. "I'm not forgetting about my dad. I'm just letting go of who I was trying to make him. I kinda like the coffee-breath version that I remember

249

anyway. It makes him human. But that's not it. I've got to tell you something else."

He blinks hard and his next words come out fast. "I told my mom everything. The itching powder. The gas pump. I'm sorry. It's just...she asked. And I said I wouldn't lie for you. But then I lied *to* you. I'm so sorry."

"Jesse, it's okay."

He shifts from one foot to the other. "I mean, I told her *all* the details."

"I know. She told my parents."

Jesse cringes. "So are you mad?"

I shrug. "Why did you do it?"

"I thought I was doing the right thing. I swear. I thought you didn't know what you were doing. Plus, my mom talked to Mr. Amondo. She already knew most of it."

"Okay."

"Okay? What do you mean?"

"I mean it's okay. That I'm not mad. That I get why you did it. Thanks for looking out for me."

Jesse hugs me. Hard. I don't think he even means to because he looks as shocked as I am when he lets go. "Thanks," he says. "I was afraid you'd be mad again."

"Brought something for the pile," Brandon says, walking up with an Xbox in his hands.

Jesse shakes his head. "You can't trash that."

"Relax," Brandon says. "It's *symbolic*."

"But is it a working symbol?" Jesse asks.

Brandon tosses it onto the top of Trashcano, and a piece pops off the front. "It was."

"Dummy," Jesse says under his breath, and goes over to the pile like he's getting ready to climb it.

"Oh man," Brandon says. "He's going to be more fun to mess with than you were."

"You know," I say to Brandon as we watch Jesse try to get his footing. "I was thinking about your story from when we first started hanging out. The one about the ants and the grasshopper?"

Brandon glances at me and then focuses on Jesse again. "Yeah?" He crosses his arms.

"I keep thinking the grasshopper was probably lonely—you know, with no other grasshoppers around. And the ants were jerks, if you think about it. They should have invited him into their hill to begin with. Maybe he'd have taught the ants to lighten up a bit."

Jesse holds up the Xbox. "Got it!" He starts climbing down.

"Basically, the ants should have made sure the grasshopper knew he was one of them, ant or not."

"Are you getting all metaphorical on me?"

"Nah. I was just thinking."

"So"—Brandon leans in—"do you think the big and strong and clever grasshopper should tell the teeny, tiny ant the Xbox actually doesn't work?"

I bow my head so Jesse can't see me laughing. "I honestly never know what the grasshopper will do next."

The guy from the junkyard left one beat-up truck out of the pile so we could use the bed as a stage during our attempt. With no wheels, it sits with its belly on the concrete. Mom, Dad, and a lady I don't know are standing in front of the makeshift stage now. When Mom sees us walking up, she waves us over and tells us to come meet today's adjudicator, Amanda Jensen.

After I shake her hand, Ms. Jensen says, "Nice to finally meet you, Milo Moss," she says. "I'm impressed with everything you've done."

I smile. "Thanks. We've had lots of practice."

"Ready to go up?" Dad asks Mom. He puts his hand on my shoulder and squeezes. "Milo, you wait with Ms. Jensen. Your mother and I will bravely scale the depths of Trashcano."

"Oh, come on." Mom grabs his arm and pulls him away.

I get onto the truck bed with Ms. Jensen. Jesse and Brandon don't follow me at first, but I tell them to come up too.

Jesse and I avoid the microphone, but Brandon walks up to it, spreads his arms wide, and says, "Thank you, Dallas, Texas!"

People stop talking, probably thinking we're officially starting. Brandon says, much quieter this time, "Oh, I didn't think that'd work so well."

The entire crowd stares at us now. Seems like most of the school is here, so are tons of people from all over Dallas. Mom and Dad told me they've met several people from other cities and even other states. Lots of them found out about the attempt from the same online board we've always used.

Allie told Jesse he would be the presenter after he was the first to say, "Not it." She said he needed to challenge himself. I think maybe Allie was worried she'd get stuck with the job.

"Thank you all for coming today," Jesse says into the microphone. "Please welcome Ms. Jensen, who is an adjudicator from Guinness. She's here to verify our record." He waits for the clapping to stop before he continues. "Now, if you'll turn your attention to the volcano, it is about to erupt."

My parents are already halfway up the enormous pile. They are riding on a cherry picker—a huge machine with a platform that rises. Dad waves to the crowd and yells, "See you on the other side," as they are lifted at a glacial pace.

Once they get to the peak, Mom and Dad dump two trash cans full of liquid nitrogen and Ping-Pong balls into the oversized, poorly welded cake pan resting at the top—except this time we've learned from experience. The poorly welded cake pan now has a plastic liner, so it doesn't leak. After they finish, Dad yells, "Coming down! Look out below!"

The mechanical hum of the cherry picker is the only sound we hear as we watch. My parents make it all the way back down and climb into the back of the truck to stand next to Jesse, Brandon, Ms. Jensen, and me.

Mom puts her arms around Dad and me while we watch, waiting for Trashcano to erupt, and for us to finally get our record.

But nothing happens.

So we wait longer.

Still nothing.

"Um, maybe we got bum nitrogen?" Dad says.

Mom frowns. "Maybe it just takes a while?"

After another few minutes, somebody in the crowd yells, "Is that it?"

Jesse's eyes are huge. He's panicking. He steps away from the microphone.

Brandon rolls his eyes but says, "I got you, man." He takes Jesse's place as the announcer and walks up to the microphone. "So this is awkward. Should we kill time by figuring out who put the most embarrassing thing into the pile? Because I saw an adult bike with training wheels. And I'm pretty sure there's a pair of underwear on the other side. But the best thing is probably the toupee." He peers over the crowd. "I see lots of shiny heads out there that it could belong to."

"It'll be fine," Jesse whispers to me, covering the mic with his hand.

"Hey, Milo." Brandon leans toward me and whispers. "Have you ever considered the fact that you're definitely cursed?"

"There's basically no other explanation," I whisper back.

I look at the adjudicator, at my mom, dad, and sister. At Mr. Amondo, Jesse, and Brandon. At all the people who are part of our own Trashcano.

I step forward. "It appears as though we are not breaking a record today," I say into the microphone. "And, I guess you could say since Trashcano is a failure, maybe this is how we get our win. We learn from our mistakes and we keep going. We choose what defines us."

Jesse steps up next to me. He starts the slow clap. My parents and Allie join him, but they are the only ones. Brandon just stands there, staring.

Then a Ping-Pong ball shoots out of the top of the mountain. And another and another, until our Trashcano is fully erupting.

I don't even think about it. I clap. I yell. I whoop. I don't know if they understand this win, but for me, after all the attempts and my previous losses, this changes everything.

"Congratulations!" says the adjudicator. "Welcome to Guinness!"

I almost can't believe it. The plaque is really mine.

And, yeah, I would have been okay if I didn't get the record.

But standing here right now: It's officially amazing.

ACKNOWLEDGMENTS

There are several Officially Amazing people I want to thank:

Guinness World Records for creating a way to celebrate differences, grit, and perseverance. And for making it fun!

John Rudolph, my agent, for rescuing my manuscript from the slush pile, seeing Milo's potential, and chiseling my work until it was no longer an epic fail.

Samantha Gentry, my editor, who loved Milo from the beginning and knew exactly how to hone my words into the story I wanted to tell. And to those at Little, Brown Books for Young Readers: Megan Tingley, Jackie Engel, Alvina Ling, Sasha Illingworth, Jenny Kimura, Marisa Finkelstein, Katharine McAnarney, Stefanie Hoffman, Mara Brashem, Savannah Kennelly, and Christie Michel. I cannot imagine a better team and home for Milo.

My friends and colleagues. The Writer's Path peeps,

especially Suzanne Frank, Pamela McManus Stiehler, and Michelle Staubach Grimes, for your encouragement and your belief that I can do this writing thing. PCE and the neighborhood for your support and excitement with all things book related. Sara Goodman for being my brain twin and sounding board for all things writing and otherwise.

My beta readers. Kristie Frazier, you have no idea how good you are at editing, so I am announcing it publicly. Kate Wallace, you read for me in the midst of uncertainty, and I am so thankful for you. Brandon Davenport, thank you for laughing at "life events," for dropping everything to help me, and for being my first fan. Brooke Fossey, you are basically part of all categories: beta reader, emergency reader, colleague, friend, and (chosen) family. Mom, I sure miss *you* when I'm gone. And to my Mimi. Your proofreading skills are unmatched—as are you!

My Westwood family. Cindy Edwards, you are the best teacher and mentor—and responder to texts that may or may not be subpoenaed in the future. Super 7's, y'all are World's Greatest Coworkers! All the kiddos of G107, thank you for letting me teach you and for letting me geek out about literature. Also for sharing your must-read books and teaching me popular slang. I'm not throwing shade or spilling tea: Brah and Sis, y'all are lit! That's a mood. No cap! (Nailed it, right?!)

My family for putting up with me and for not being mad at me when I can't play games because I have to edit (or sleep).

My kids, Colton, Logan, and Rowyn, who provide me with endless story inspiration. I might be able to write faster if you weren't so noisy, but I wouldn't laugh and love as much. Being your mom is my ultimate win.

My husband, Zach. Thank you for being my partner in all attempts at life. There is nobody I'd rather fail or win with than you.

Chemenn Photography

LAUREN ALLBRIGHT

is the author of the middle-grade novel *Exit Strategy*. When she is not writing (or failing in her attempts at Mom of the Year), she teaches seventh graders who might earn a record for some of the World's Coolest Kids Ever. She lives in Dallas with her awesome husband and her three epic children.